The Undrowning Lotus

A WW2 Historical Novel,
Based on a True Story
of a Sexual Slavery Survivor

Pacific Atrocities Education

The Undrowning Lotus

A WW2 Historical Novel,
Based on a True Story
of a Sexual Slavery Survivor

Jenny Chan

The Undrowning Lotus

A WW2 Historical Novel,
Based on a True Story
of a Sexual Slavery Survivor

Cover Illustration:
Ana Jakić Divković

Editor:
Barbara Halperin

Publisher:
Pacific Atrocities Education
730 Commercial Street
San Francisco, CA 94108

For more info on this book
and comfort women survivors, check out
https://www.pacificatrocities.org/
book-the-undrowning-lotus.html

Paperback ISBN: 978-1-947766-28-0

E-book ISBN: 978-1-947766-14-3

Table of Contents

Chapter 1

"YOUR NAME IS Wang Chunhua. You were born on the 12th day of the twelfth lunar month in 1929. Your birthplace is Jiucaigou Village, Helingeer County, Suiyuan Province. Your father's name is Wang Dahai and your mother's name is Zhang Hong. You have an older brother, a younger brother, and two younger sisters."

As we walked up a rocky path, Niang repeated this to me, looking worried that I would forget our family details. As a harsh wind blew, Niang continued expressing her concerns.

"The winter is coming. Good thing I put more clothes on you this morning. But I am sure your new family will be able to provide more than we could ever provide you."

If I had known this was going to be the last time I would see Niang, I would have hugged her harder and convinced her to go with me or for me to stay. But I did not. She had always been there for the family and me.

"I am heading back to the farm to do more harvesting," said Niang, as she took one last look at me. "You better come home right after you take care of this, and don't even think about using the money on opium," said Niang sternly to Papa.

"Yes, I promise," said Papa. This was not the first time Papa said these words. I had heard them repeatedly over the last couple years. I heard Niang demanding him to work last week and his answer was exactly the same.

I took a good look at Papa, standing here waiting with me. He had aged so much in the last year. Since the New Year, he had been going to the den in the center of town to smoke opium. It started as a social celebration with his friends but, very soon, it became a regular habit.

"Why don't you help me out in planting the seeds? Do you think food is going to grow itself?" asked Niang in the spring.

"I just need to entertain my friends," said Papa.

"You have been entertaining for years."

"Only a few months. This is why I need my friends. They are more objective and they do not talk about exaggerated things like you," replied Papa as he walked out.

A few months ago, Niang gave birth to my younger brother. Nainai came from another village to help her, while Papa still sat in the den in the daytime. Due to Nainai's age, she could not work as hard in the field as Niang. A week after my younger brother was born, Niang returned to the field while Nainai took care of us.

"Would it be better if Papa was dead?" I asked Niang during dinner one day.

"Don't say that; he is still your biological father."

"But he is not Papa anymore. I do not know who he is anymore. He has not worked in the field. He is eating our portions of the food and he has not played with us for months."

One night, I heard Niang crying to Nainai.

"We are out of money. He just stole from the drawer again."

Nainai held Niang trying to comfort her as Niang continued to cry. Papa returned home demanding to be fed.

"Why is dinner still not ready yet?"

"Because you took our last penny for your opium. Do you even see the family in your eyes?"

"I can return in a few days with some money and food," said Nainai.

In a few days, Nainai returned with food and some money and saw Papa lying in bed staring into space.

"My daughter has been working the hardest for you. Are you even planning to take care of her and my grand-children?" asked Nainai.

"Your daughter and your grandchildren are my property. What I do with them is none of your business," answered Papa.

Nainai never returned and our family became even more desperate. Last week, while we were sitting around the wobbly table eating our usual corn gruel, Niang asked "Can you help with the field tomorrow? It is the beginning of the harvesting season. I could use some help."

"You are very annoying," answered Papa.

"But we are out of money, and..."

"We can just sell Chunhua," interrupted Papa.

"Why? She is our daughter and she is only four!" screamed Niang.

"Well, do you want us to sell our son instead? At least we can pretend Chunhua is eight years old. Look at how tall she is. At least we could sell her to some family who could feed her."

"What if she gets married to someone like you?" asked Niang.

"What's wrong with being like me?"

"The days are shorter, and we cannot even afford to get wood to start a fire," complained Niang. Papa ignored her, demanding to have dinner. Niang fought with Papa the entire week before Niang finally agreed after Papa promised to never entertain his friends nor smoke again.

"This time, I really promise," Papa confirmed.

I grew worried as I waited for the vendor to pick me up. I had heard many gruesome stories about children who were sold in this village, but I never thought my day would come. My friend, Meiling, came by my home two months ago to say goodbye to me before the vendor picked her up.

"Where are you going?" I asked.

"Not sure. Maybe I will be a slave in the south. Maybe a family will buy me as a wife for their dead son."

Papa turned to me and said, "Don't worry, you are a strong child. You will survive."

I dared not reply. I hated this man so much, but I really wished that he would be a changed man after I am sold.

Finally, a woman with crooked yellow teeth showed up. Her hands were clean unlike Niang's rough earthly hands. I could tell this woman had never farmed a day in her life.

"How old is she?" asked the woman.

"Eight," lied Papa.

"Hmm. She is not pretty but not bad looking either," commented the woman. She looked me up and down and I could tell that she was examining me.

"Why are her feet not bound if she is eight years old?"

"We are peasants," answered my father.

"Even the servants in the south have bound feet. I cannot pay you a high amount without bound feet."

The lady counted some coins and handed them to Papa. Papa stared at his hand, counted and happily told me to behave myself.

The roads up the mountain were bumpy. I was hungry from traveling, but was too worried about my future to have any appetite. During the night, we were handed a blanket with some water and bread to share. I felt hungry but was too nervous to bring the bread to my mouth. I stared at the steamed bun in front of me, imagining what Niang was up to right now. Could my siblings finally be full now from the food bought with money earned from selling me?

"Are you going to eat that?" asked the girl next to me.

"Not sure," I replied.

"What do you mean not sure? You better not waste any food. Food is scarce on the road."

"Well, do you want it?" I asked.

"Absolutely!"

She shoved the steamed bun greedily into her mouth. I regretted my decision as I watched her finishing even the crumbs.

"Thank you so much!" The girl expressed her gratitude as she wiped her mouth with her sleeve.

"Do you know where we are going?" I asked.

"No idea. I have been on the road for quite a while now. Not sure when the next meal is going to come. But this is still better than staying at home."

"Why? What is happening at home?"

"No water. There is no food. There is a famine happening," answered the girl.

"That is also happening in my village," I said.

"I just hope that we are not going to run into bandits," the girl continued.

"What?"

"I heard from the last vendor that a group of bandits attacked her group and snatched a few children like us."

"Oh, is this why we need to darken our faces like this?"

"Yes, and she heard that the children are being used as servants and the more mature ones are now concubines for the top bandit."

I tried to listen to her, but I had enough of my own worries to think about. I tried to hide how tired I was, but my body let out a yawn.

"You must be tired. We did travel for a whole day," said the girl.

I nodded and as we slept on the floor, I woke up from hunger a few times in the middle of the night.

The harsh wind blew from the western Mongolian desert at night as we approached our rest stops. I was hoping this would be the last time to be handed to a new vendor. It was awkward each and every time I was handed to a new person. I started eavesdropping on the vendors' conversations at the rest stops and learned I was being traded for more money each and every time. The girl who shared my food was long gone a few rest stops ago. At the first rest station, there was a woman begging to be sold with her youngest daughter. I can still remember the cries, more desperate than I had ever heard.

"My daughter does not need much to survive on. Just half a bowl of congee per day. Please! Just let me be sold with her!"

The vendor nodded, "Even if I sell you with her right now, I cannot guarantee that you could both be sold together next time."

As I was passed from vendor to vendor, each trying to make an extra penny out of me, I started feeling like an object.

By the fourth rest stop, I had forgotten my name. I stayed silent when the buyer asked for my name.

"Come on, you can talk, prove it," the seller told me impatiently.

"Anyway, I can promise that she is not mute. And look at how strong she is. You get what you paid for." The seller then turned to me and punched my stomach so hard that I screamed.

"See, told you, she is not mute." She then collected money off the buyer.

When we arrived at Fen River for a rest stop, I saw a herd of sheep next to the freshest water I have ever seen. The valley next to the river was lush.

"Healthy sheep!" exclaimed Miu, the seller.

"Yes, I can sell one to you for a silver," the herder replied.

"What about a set of them for a girl?"

"Deal."

The vendor traded me for a pair of sheep. I followed the herder home.

"Do we need another mouth to feed?" asked his wife when he showed me to her.

"No, but can you dress her up and we can bring her to Taiyuan to sell? With her strong build, we could probably sell her for more than a pair of skinny sheep. If we clean her and put a new shirt on her, she could be worth two silvers."

She washed me that night, her gentle touch reminding me of Niang. She then put a red dress on me.

"Are you hungry? They must not have fed you for a while."

"Yes."

She gave me half a bowl of congee mixture. It had been awhile since I tasted any warm food and I shed a tear in joy.

The next day, we traveled to Taiyuan. There were many stores in the streets and buildings with clay roofs and wooden doors were very popular. A fancy looking restaurant had women in skimpy clothes luring men in fancy silk suits to enter. There were donkeys pulling wagons everywhere. A special kind of excitement filled the streets as street vendors busily sold corn, pumpkins and wheat. A person with blue eyes, gold hair and too short for his height was standing at the street corner with a book shouting, "God will forgive your sins. Jesus is your savior."

"Why does he look like that?" I asked the herder's wife.

"Don't look at him! He is a white devil who believes a man nailed on a cross is a savior. But do you know why the man is on the cross?"

"No."

"My relative told me white devils like that built a church in the town and they started worshiping Jesus, a bastard born by an unclean woman. The statue blocked the blessing from heaven and her town was raided by a Japanese expedition force right after the church was built! Avoid eye contact with the white devil! It might bring you bad luck!"

She brought me to an alley where an old lady met us and enthusiastically offered two silvers for me. "Won't a family be excited to have you as a child bride!" The old lady brought me to a small hut in the middle of a valley that night where we met three other girls that she kept waiting there. We traveled together for a few days until we came to Yangquan Village in the Yu County of Shanxi Province. By the time we arrived, the red dress I was wearing was already filled with dirt and my hair was gelled by oil.

The village was filled with brown mud-brick houses with arched wooden doorways and rows of houses on the rocky hills. The grey roofs looked like they were floating individually but they fit in with each other very harmoniously. The brown mountains in the background looked deserted, as if there was a drought. "There are some families who need wives in this village," said the lady who brought the girls to the village. She then brought us into a store right inside the town's gate where we washed and were given new dresses.

Chapter 2

WHEN WE ARRIVED, Yangquan was going through one of the worst famines in Chinese history. The village looked deserted since many had fled to nearby Taiyuan for jobs building railroads. We walked through winding roads between houses before we reached the first house to drop off the first girl. We were told to wait outside while the seller walked with the girl into her new household. We waited nervously, for what felt like a lifetime, while judging the dire situation of the village.

The seller began telling us of our fortunate situation. "This is the first time in months where a group of bandits did not kidnap our child brides. You could end up in horrible situations if that had happened. A bandit would make all of you his wives or slaves. You will all be brides in good families. So you better behave well. Let me tell all of you about etiquette."

"You must not talk too much when you meet the new in-laws. Always let the husband or his family speak first.

If not, there will be consequences. Work hard and do not speak too much," continued the seller.

Looking at the fields ahead of us, as though she just remembered a thought, she murmured, "Women are like grass, born to be stepped on."

As we walked through the village, I looked at the farms around us which were in far worse condition than the village where I was born. In comparison, mother's farm looked somewhat healthier. The stalks of corn that survived were orange and fragile looking. Flocks of sheep looked as though they were starving as they climbed up the naked hills across the fields. I was increasingly nervous when it was my turn to be dropped off. We walked through a pair of wooden doors into a courtyard that had a pile of squash in the middle. There was an old lady right in front of me staring into the courtyard through a set of opened windows made of rice paper and wood.

"That old lady is your new grandmother-in-law," said the seller, as if she read my mind.

We walked up the grey concrete stairwell into the door with rice paper windows. The old lady looked as if she had been impatiently waiting.

"Sorry, Mrs. Li to keep you waiting."

The old lady sipped from her tea cup and nodded.

"I believe this is a girl strong enough for your farm. What do you think?" asked the seller.

"How old is she?" The old lady questioned with a concerned face.

"Nine," answered the seller.

"Well, our Wuxiao is only 7. Isn't she a bit too old?"

"You know, I was focused on picking only the strongest girls for Yangquan Village. A normal girl from the south would not survive here," answered the seller defensively.

"Fine. But what kind of family is she from? Why are her feet still unbound at the age of nine?"

"If she was from a well-to-do family, she would not be here right now. You would not be able to get her at such a reasonable price. But at least she fit what your astrologist told me to find to match your grandson's fate."

After the seller left, Mrs. Li brought Wuxiao out. Wuxiao was smaller than me. He was staring at the floor as Mrs. Li told him, "This will be your new wife in a few days." According to Mrs. Li, I was still not a part of the family yet. In Chinese tradition, it was unlucky to see your spouse before the wedding. In order to prevent me from seeing Wuxiao, she ordered me to sleep in the barn next to the donkey. I was also ordered to not talk to other men in the fields or around the village. Winter was coming, but there was only a little coal prepared for me to keep warm so I could stay alive. After a little over a year of traveling, I was so grateful to finally settle somewhere.

It was hard for me to adapt to sleeping in the cold barn since the coal takes a while to heat up the surface of the kang. Sometimes the wind seeping through the door woke me up in the middle of the night. Eventually, my body was able to adapt and I was able to sleep through the night. I had weird dreams in the barn. I dreamed of the days when I was at home with my family, still playing with my younger sisters while Niang was harvesting. On the way home from the fields, we were robbed by a group of bandits. Once we got home, Papa was so mad at Niang and us that he decided to sell all of us. I always woke up in the middle of the night hoping that my sisters and Niang were okay. There were nights when I could not fall asleep because I felt anxious about my family at home.

Mrs. Li changed my name to Kuaishou on the day of the wedding. "According to the astrologist, that name is more lucky for our field. It means quick hand, meaning, you will work quickly in the field and bring us crops," explained Mrs. Li.

"From now on, you are Li Kuaishou. You need to remember that your behavior reflects our family."

On the morning of the wedding, the whole house smelled like incense. Mrs. Li woke up early that morning to have a ceremony to pray to all kinds of Gods. She was praying to the Gate God, the God for Underground, the God of Mercy, and others. She started preparing for the feast for the entire week. She called in help from other ladies all over the village and they all were cooking outside the house. All the coal stoves were occupied with pots and woks.

"You are lucky. Our village has not had a feast like this in months," said Mrs. Li.

The entire village was invited to the banquet. My head was covered by a red cloth and a headdress. A village lady told me to sit down with Wuxiao in the front of the courtyard. As we were waiting, grandma was cutting a roasted lamb to be divided among and shared with the villagers. Wuxiao then lifted the red cloth on my headdress so we could eat. Our table was filled with food. Grandma was right; I was lucky to be here for a feast. I had never seen so much food in my life. The table was filled with steamed chicken, part of a roasted lamb, dumplings, hand-pulled noodles, and the famous northern dish called three roots from the ground, which is made of eggplants, potatoes and green peppers.

After the meal, Grandma escorted us to our new bedroom. It felt luxurious compared to the barn where I had been sleeping. The room had red linen bedding with sewn dragon and phoenix designs. There was a set of red curtains right outside the bed and next to it was a table with a pair of red candles. Wuxiao seemed shy while he stood next to me.

"Grandma told me to do my best to pass on our genes," said Wuxiao. This was the first time I had ever heard Wuxiao talking. I nodded recalling what the seller told me; a woman should not talk that much. Wuxiao pulled a book out of his sleeve to show me what he meant.

"According to my grandma, this is what we need to do to continue our family," said Wuxiao as he put the book on the wooden table next to the red candles. His face was blushing as red as the candles. I took a look at the cover. It was an old blue cover with the title, "Autumn Blossoming Pictures." Then I flipped through and it was full of naked pictures of people. I immediately started blushing.

"We can try," I stated, not even sure how we could get started. In my mind, I was worried. I had nothing in common with this guy. This was the first time we ever shared a conversation. Yet, we were married. Supposedly, he is my family member now. We shared a bed that night. Though we had nothing in common, we both accepted fate, as this is what China had done to its children for many generations.

The next morning, I woke up to the sound of roosters. Wuxiao was still deep asleep next to me. It was the first night in a month that I was warm enough to get a full night of sleep. The new bed I had was not too comfortable, but at least it was warm. I reported to my new Nainai. She looked exhausted from the wedding feast, which made her look older than usual.

"Now that you are a part of the Li family, it is my duty to educate you as the head of the household," Nainai Li stated.

"Judging that you are a country bumpkin from Mongolia, I bet that you do not know about the seven unacceptable behaviors, according to Confucius, of being a daughter-in-law."

I stayed silent as she continued speaking.

"Number one, you cannot commit any impious act. Technically, as your grandma-in-law, I have more power over you than your own mother. Second, you cannot be childless. You need a son to continue our Li bloodline. Third, you cannot commit adultery. I do not want to hear about your affairs with other men. Fourth, no acts of jealousy. If my grandson decided to have a concubine, to expand our bloodline, you cannot be jealous of the concubine. Fifth, you cannot be sick. Sixth, you cannot speak your own mind. Seventh, you cannot steal from the family and use our resources for yourself. Do you understand?" I nodded.

She continued, "But there are exceptions. If you no longer have a family to return to or if you had been a widow for three years or if you are our lucky charm causing us to be wealthy."

I thought I fit into the category of not having a family to return to, but I dared not interrupt.

"And you are going to follow me to the fields today. We don't have money to feed another idle mouth."

Chapter 3

"WINTER IS OVER SOON," Li Nainai stated at dinner one day.

"Yes, Nainai, and we are getting the field ready for spring planting," I replied.

Wuxiao and I stopped eating to pay attention to her. I grew nervous as I knew what she was about to propose.

"I know. And we should bind your feet before spring comes so they are less likely to be infected."

The next morning, she came to my room with a brown bucket containing a brown mixture of sheep blood and herbs. I was instructed to soak my feet in the bucket. Li Nainai stepped out and came back to my room with cloth and wire. She sat on the floor, held onto my left foot with her left hand and began wrapping it with wire. It was so painful, I could not help but scream, but he shushed me.

"Can you stop screaming? This is for your own good."

I heard my bones cracking as I tried to bite my lips shut.

She did the same thing to my right foot. As she wrapped, I could not help but scream and she started shouting at me.

"Why are you so dramatic? Women have done this for thousands of years. I have bound feet. So does my mother, my grandmother and my grandmother's grandmother," she shouted. I could feel her wrapping my feet tighter as she was shouting.

"You could have bed rest tonight. I do not know what kind of family raised you. You are not supposed to let your in-laws bind your feet."

I laid there thinking about what she told me. For centuries, Chinese women had suffered. Why is there no end to this torture?

Spring time came and the frost was disappearing from the ground. It was time to start with full time work in the field again since my feet were healing from the initial binding a month earlier. But there was no time to waste; I had to learn how to walk all over again and start working. My feet felt numb as I touched the floor for the first time after a week of bedrest but there was no other way around not working. As Li Nainai said, "The Li family does not have spare resources to feed an extra idle mouth." In the field, I had to be overly careful. My feet were sometimes infected as dirt from the earth got into the bandages as I worked. I needed to be as careful as possible as I sowed seeds in the ground. If the infection got bad, pus flowed through bandages to the earth beneath me.

I was behind the ox everyday plowing the fields. Sometimes, Li Nainai requested that I walk 10 lis[*] to neighboring villages to get coal. My stomach started to become upset from being so hungry all the time and I started eating more during dinner. During dinner one night, Li Nainai started questioning my appetite.

"Why are you eating so much? Wuxiao only eats one bowl of congee a day."

"She works as much as our ox does," answered Wuxiao, defending me. Then he poured some food from his bowl into my bowl. Wuxiao had been a lot warmer to me since we first met at our wedding.

After dinner, I thanked him for standing up for me. "No problem. Sometimes she is hard to deal with. My father died because of her." Then he stopped talking, but I could tell that something was bothering him.

"I know I am not supposed to ask, but what happened to your parents?"

Wuxiao started sobbing. It was the first time I had ever seen him this upset. I rubbed his back to comfort him.

"I found my father dead on the floor last summer. Before he died, I remember Nainai telling him, 'You are so lazy, I wish you were dead so we don't need to feed another lazy mouth.' And the next day, he was dead," continued Wuxiao.

"What did he die from?" I asked.

"Opium," answered Wuxiao. I was silent thinking about my own father.

---

[*] Li is Chinese unit of measurement. 1 li = 415.8 meters.

"My mother was married into the house as a slave. Back then, our family was still doing well. I know it is hard to imagine, but we had a lot more workers in the field. Then my father fell in love with my mother and they got married."

"But of course, Nainai thought Papa should have married someone else to improve our family standing in the village, but Papa ended up marrying a slave with normal feet. Then Nainai and Papa were arguing every night."

"Not long after their marriage, the famine began. Many of the friendly villagers came to loot us because they heard that we had food in our shed," continued Wuxiao. "Soon, Papa was seeking to escape from the real world. He became addicted to opium, the only social activity he participated in with his friends. Our fields were left unplowed. The famine came. Some fields were sold to other people in order for us to survive. After Papa passed away, Nainai decided to sell my mother, thinking that she is unlucky and was the reason why all of this happened."

"That is why there is only you and Nainai," I whispered.

"Our family used to be a lot bigger. I told Nainai that I would go to my mother's place, but I was supposed to stay home to continue the bloodline," Wuxiao said, finishing the story. This was the first time I have ever heard him talk for this long.

In the morning, I made breakfast for the whole family. During the day, I plowed the field with the ox. Sometimes I went to another village to get coal. In the evening after dinner, I took out the bucket of waste from the outhouse.

Sometimes I sat out in the field in the middle of the day to wonder about life. What is the meaning of my life? Would I be living like this for the rest of my life? Pain, labor, and all?

I took a look at my feet. I could feel them curling toward the ground. Maybe that is why bound feet are called Golden Lilies? While looking at my feet, I saw a group of my neighbors gathering below in their field.

For the next few weeks, the group slowly increased in size. I wanted to join them but was in fear of my Li Nainai catching me. I could only watch from afar. These were the most hopeful people I had seen for a while. I could hear them chanting from a distance. They were acting as if the famine did not exist and there was no daily labor. Their hopefulness really sparked excitement in me. Finally, I was ready to ask Wuxiao to join me for these meetings. During dinner, I pretended that everything was normal out in the field.

"How was the field? Did the ice dissolve yet?" Grandma asked in a suspicious voice.

"Everything is good."

After dinner, I told Wuxiao what I had seen in the field. His eyes widened and asked, "Do you want to join?"

"Of course!"

In the morning, I felt motivated to get up and do chores. The thought of meeting with a group of enthusiastic people our age gave me energy I had never felt before. My life was suddenly filled with hope again. I felt as if I did chores much faster than usual. I ran to the Ma River as quickly as I could with everyone's clothes and rapidly scrubbed them on the board. I was more motivated than ever to finish the tasks at hand and was intrigued about what was going to happen in the afternoon. In the afternoon, midway through planting seeds, Wuxiao came to the field to meet me.

"Are you ready?"

I nodded.

We walked down the hills. I saw our neighbors herding goats and was nervous about the situation.

"What if we were seen by our neighbors?"

"You are with your husband. We were just going for a walk if they asked," answered Wuxiao.

I was excited to finally see the group up close. They looked like such young energetic people, like my age, and they seemed to have purpose in their lives. One of them shouted, "Down with the capitalist pigs." I looked around and saw an attractive girl with two pigtails. She noticed me staring and glanced back at me. I felt my face heating up and immediately looked away.

Chapter 4

L I NAINAI PACED BACK and forth in the living room nervously as she chatted with the servant. "Do we have enough to pay taxes this year?"

The servant replied, "I doubt it, but I can skip my salary this quarter."

Li Nainai said "How can I do that to you? You are already our last servant in our household. You have skipped your salary for the last year."

"Without the Li family, my life would not exist. Remember how you saved me from my starving village? My family had no choice but to sell me. You made an offer to my family and saved my life! And if you don't make the payment to our government, they will send the local enforcement group to confiscate the whole Li household."

"What had the government done for us? They defeated the warlords, but the taxes we have to pay now are much higher than what the warlords used to charge us!"

"Well, they did send enforcements here to make our village safer. Ever since the government added more local enforcements, the bandits are afraid to rob the merchants. Kuaishou would have never made it to our family if there were bandits along the way. Remember how other child brides were taken by bandits along the way?"

"So, the plan is to save as much money as possible until tax day."

"Yes, our government needs our money to get ready for the war with the Japanese. While getting supplies in Taiyuan, I heard that Japan had already captured Manchuria and started training their army there. A war with the whole country of China is going to happen sooner or later."

"What a time to be alive!" As Li Nainai exclaimed, she realized that Wuxiao and I were listening to their conversation.

"Kuaishou, why don't you get to the field so we could have a great harvest this year to pay for our taxes?" asked Li Nainai.

"I will go with her as well," answered Wuxiao before I had the chance to reply.

"Why are you so eager to come to the field with me today?" I asked Wuxiao as we were walking to the field.

"I want to see our comrades," and his eyes lit up as he was describing the young Communists in the field.

In the afternoon, the group of comrades arrived at the field. The leader of the group was named Wang Liye.

"The leader of our party is getting us ready for war with the Japanese devils," stated Liye.

"I thought the Guomindang were going to fight them," interrupted Wuxiao.

"Great comment, comrade! What is your name?"

"Wuxiao."

"Are you new?"

"Yes."

"Oh, this is why you are so clueless. General Chiang in Guomindang only knows how to fundraise to expand his soldiers. But the generals working under him and the government are corrupt. When it comes to fighting, they are not as genuine as Comrade Mao. Comrade Mao focuses on real training instead of fancy strategy and money like Guomindang. Comrade Mao started a training program for our party to learn how to defend ourselves to form a strong country. I was fortunate to be able to train with his troop in the cold mountain."

"What is Comrade Mao like?" I asked comrade Liye.

"He has a gentle soul. You can tell from his eyes that he cares deeply about us peasants. He has a tendency toward tough love. He made us sleep on pillows made from our own shirts and demonstrated how to do it himself. During training in the snow, he jokingly told us to take off all of our shirts so we could roll in the snow. At first, we all thought he was joking, but he demonstrated how to do it in front of us. All of us were surprised and we decided to follow his example. He is definitely a leader who leads by actions, which is why all of us respect him. Are you and Wuxiao interested in following him as well?"

Wuxiao and I nodded simultaneously. I was a bit nervous about joining the training with my bound feet but, at the same time, was excited about the possibility. I was mostly impressed by how I could express myself freely in public in this new movement.

The girl with pigtails became my mentor for the training. Her name was Dong E, which meant winter lady. She had recently married into the village just like me. She must have been the best looking woman in the whole village. Her face reminded me of the doll Niang bought me. I heard from the other girls in the unit that, like many other women, she was also married as a child bride at the age of 15. During training, we often exchanged looks as if we understood each other without a word. I later found out that I was not the only one who thought she was the best looking person in the village. Her nickname was "Kai Shanxi", which means the best look of Shanxi. She reminded me on a regular basis why we were having a revolution.

"Our country is sick, and instead of treating it with medicine, we are putting outdated herbal medicine in it. Things need to change. We are living in a shell of our country's glorious past," stated Dong E repeatedly. She and her husband became involved in the revolution a couple of years ago when her husband's uncle started leading the revolution of the community party.

Liye secretly taught all of us how to read, including the girls. We all learned eagerly, but we promised to pretend as if we did not know how to read when we were at home. Hell would break loose if Li Nainai knew that I learned how to read. The literature we learned was from the popular Chairman Mao.

"Arranged marriage is indirectly raping your own child," Liye explained to us.

"This means all of us comrades have been raped by our parents," I shouted, and everyone laughed uncomfortably.

"Correct. This is why we need our revolution."

Liye thought hard for an example and continued.

"Our leader, Mao, had tried to work together with our current system, but when the past president, Sun Yat-sen, passed away in March 1925, the whole country seemed to be shocked. Modern China was not ready to go forward without a strong compassionate leader, and Chiang Kai-shek was not the best leader for us. In April, 1927, Chiang Kai-shek led an army to kill us Communists and continued to work with foreigners. Despite the fact that we are all Chinese, he was brutal. Of course, the Communists lost a lot of party members and lost as our party is not as well equipped as Guomingdang's. In September, Chairman Mao led a Long March into Jiangxi County. He was then voted by most of us to become our leader. He reorganized us and taught us how to fight better wars. 'We might not have as many resources as our government, but we have the heart and soul to fight for a better future for this country.' His words convinced us to fight and organize our own troops and, as a leader, he instilled discipline in us. He is ready to punish any of us who violate the party laws. This way, he can trust us to organize our troops where we come from. I am ready to die for a leader like Chairman Mao."

The whole class cheered at Liye's speech.

Every evening when I returned home, I was exhausted not only from the field work, but I was also exhausted from learning the literature of the revolution. My responses from Li Nainai became slower than when I first arrived.

"What's wrong? Is everything okay?" asked Li Nainai.

"Yes. The field is doing great. It looks like we will have a great harvest this year to be able to pay our taxes," I replied.

"Wuxiao, why don't you eat more? It must be hard helping her out in the field. Look at you, your skin got a lot darker this season."

"I am okay, Ma. I am becoming a man, this is more of a manly look," Wuxiao jokingly said.

The whole table laughed when he said that.

"You are definitely getting more mature. I can't wait when you are ready to get me a grandchild." Li Nainai looked at us when she stated that.

I felt myself blushing as I tried to look as if I had not heard her and continued eating. The time had passed so quickly. It had already been two years since I was sold out of my old house. I was slowly growing into a strong girl.

The crops in the field had been growing well this season, the soybeans were already harvested by the middle of

July and the corn was orange and lively. Our servant was proud of the field and reported all to Li Nainai and her worries seemed to be relieved by the results of the field work.

"Good work, Kuaishou; our astrologist didn't name you incorrectly," Li Nainai complimented me for the first time. She then ordered the servant to take Wuxiao and I out to Taiyuan as a reward.

Chapter 5

W E REACHED THE GATE of Yangquan early in the morning after Li Nainai waved goodbye to us.

"Be careful," she said to Wuxiao, and she turned around to the servant.

"Please take care of them. Wuxiao is our only bloodline forward for the Li family."

"Are you sure you don't want to come with?" asked the servant.

"I am too old for this trip and I need to keep track of our estate in Yangquan. Not everyone is doing as well as us, and there have been reportedly many thefts happening here. We need to be careful."

"They are just poor villagers who aren't getting a bite to eat because of the poor quality of soil," replied the servant.

"I know, but there is not enough to go around to feed them. We need to keep our family alive first," said Li Nainai as she waved us off.

Using used grain bags, the servant had tied bags of goods onto the donkey. We also were wearing clothes with holes on them.

"Why are we dressed like this?" asked Wuxiao.

"We need to look like poor peasants or else groups of bandits will come out and rob us especially in these mountainous roads. They are more likely to be here," replied the servant.

"You have been in our home since I was a baby and I never knew your name. What is your name? Where are you from? Who are you? All of our servants left during the famine when we had no food for anyone except you. Why did you stay? I never had the chance to ask," Wuxiao asked these questions curiously.

The servant quietly looked at the ground.

"I was born in Tai'An Cun, not far from Taiyuan. My name at birth was Xiao Si, meaning Small Four because I was the fourth child in the family. Three of my older siblings had already died from starvation. My parents worked hard to keep me alive. My papa was a coal miner. He went to work early every morning and came back home with a miner's cough every night. During the famine in 1922, I was sold by my parents. They had no choice." She took a pause to hold in her tears. I was starting to pity her. Her times sounded worse than mine.

"They put me in a corn bag and put a handkerchief in my mouth so I would not be able to yell out loud. Then they handed me with the bag to a distant cousin living in Yangquan. That person happened to be Li Nainai."

"Li Nainai took care of me as if I was her own daughter. I worked hard in return for her saving my life. I watched the Li family being reduced during the last famine and I promised to stay to take care of her and her family no matter what happened."

"What happened to your family? Do you know?" asked Wuxiao.

"Li Nainai told me that they escaped to the mountains and were eating tree bark to survive. Eventually, they made it to Taiyuan where they became servants of a family. Sometimes, I can still hear my papa coughing at night," answered Xiao Si.

"Well, let's find them!" I excitedly answered.

Xiao Si and Wuxiao nodded in agreement.

At night, we hid in a bush and Xiao Si started a small fire to keep us warm.

"You guys must be hungry," she whispered, reaching into the bag the donkey had been carrying and giving us each a piece of bread.

"What about you?" asked Wuxiao.

"Good boy, so considerate. Your mom would be proud of you if she knew," Xiao Si stated while smiling.

Wuxiao blushed while splitting his piece of bread in half and sharing it with Xiao Si. "You have suffered enough in your life."

We all slept on the ground at night. The next day, we woke up to a nice mist over us and a nice breeze blowing in our faces.

"We are almost there. About 20 lis away," stated Xiao Si.

A group of bald men approached us from afar. A few of them wore hats and a few had headbands. They were carrying swords on their backs. Xiao Si spotted them, and told us, "Oh no, they might be bandits."

One of the bandits pointed at us with his sword, "Charge!"

Xiao Si got in front of Wuxiao, me, and the donkey, pulled out a gun she was hiding in her pants and pointed at the group of bandits.

"Be careful," said Wuxiao.

"Don't get close to us! I will shoot you," shouted Xiao Si.

"Don't you dare, bitch!" one of the bandits exclaimed.

I could feel Xiao Si trembling as she pointed toward the sky and fired the gun.

A group of people in uniform heard the gunshot and started running down the hill.

"Is everyone okay?" shouted one of the uniformed men.

The bandits started backing away. Before escaping, one of them turned around and said, "You got lucky this time. We will come back for you!"

"Thank you very much," stated Xiao Si as she bowed to express her gratitude toward the men in uniform.

"No need, it is our duty. Sorry, we were too late and they escaped. We heard numerous reports of bandits frequenting this area so we increased police patrolling around a 20 lis radius of Taiyuan," explained one of the policemen. One of the policemen offered to protect us until we reached the gate of Taiyuan and Xiao Si accepted the offer.

As we reached the gate of Taiyuan, I was reminded of the bustling city during my travels to Yangquan. I told Wuxiao how lucky we were to have survived a bandit attack.

"I didn't even know Xiao Si owned a gun," Wuxiao said to me in a confused tone.

"The times force us to extremes," I replied. I felt as if I understood Xiao Si more clearly. Being from a poor famine driven part of China during difficult times must have forced her to grow up fast. Being only less than a decade older than us, she behaved as if she was the same age as Li Nainai.

Xiao Si thanked the police again and again for bringing us to Taiyuan in safety. "Thank you so much for saving the children and me." We continued walking when we reached Taiyuan until we reached the river in the middle of the city. Xiao Si explained to us that this is where all the trading took place. She explained that selling things here would bring a higher price than if we sold our goods at Yangquan.

"This is the only way we could pay for the expensive tax."

Before we reached the area where all the merchants were, Xiao Si removed a bag from the baggage on the donkey.

"Here, change into these, so we could look like fancy merchants. That way, merchants will give us more respect and give us a higher price for our crops."

She then cleaned all of our faces so we no longer had dirt on them, transforming us into fancier merchants. Merchants near the river paid us respect as Xiao Si bargained to get us a better price.

"Where did she learn this from?" Wuxiao asked me.

I shrugged, "At least she is helping us get better prices for our crops. We worked hard and we deserve top dollar for our goods!"

At the end of the day, Xiao Si was counting with us the silver she had received for the goods. "This should be enough for the taxes as well as saving some if anything happens."

Wuxiao looked at her with confusion in his face.

"What could happen?" I asked innocently.

"A merchant told me that the Imperial Japanese soldiers had already started making their way this way. They had already occupied Manchuria a few years ago and started training their soldiers there. There are currently more Imperial Japanese soldiers in Manchuria than our own soldiers. Of course, our own soldiers decided to fight each other instead of protecting us peasants. Our lives are in our own hands. Our harvest better be good in the next season as well so we can stock up before we are invaded like Manchuria."

We walked by the missionaries in Taiyuan. I told Wu-xiao and Xiao Si what I heard regarding the people from the missionary. Xiao Si laughed at my innocence and gullibility.

"There are good and bad foreigners just like anything else. It is true that foreigners started taking over our country with wars but our own countrymen are to blame for this. Chinese people have weak minds and succumbed to the opium that the foreigners fed us, making us an easier target, if we were not easy enough." She then explained to us what the good foreigners did for our country.

"They provided education, liberated women from abusive relationships and provided jobs to the locals. Their beliefs and will power are so strong. We need to be more like them. Did you know they even stayed when the official of a Qing dynasty official ordered them to be massacred."

"Massacred?" Wuxiao asked curiously.

"About 30 years ago, our country was still a powerful dynasty with a powerful queen who wanted to advance our country. But there were many officials who were against the technological advancement that the queen suggested. The officials also did not believe that she should not have held any kind of government position because she was a woman. Yuxian, one of the high officials who was as smart as a donkey, was jealous of the foreign missionaries' popularity and ordered them to be killed. He brought a mob to violently attack them and ordered all of them to be executed at once. I heard from

Li Nainai that all of Shanxi was rained on then. It was as if heaven was crying that the last attempt at saving us Chinese people was going to be blocked by a corrupt official." The tales of the Chinese are just examples of how easily we could be manipulated as a people.

Chapter 6

L I NAINAI WAS SURPRISED to hear of the bandits attack and our adventures in Taiyuan. She rewarded Xiao Si with an extra bowl of noodles for being able to sell our items for a higher price than she imagined as well as protecting us.

"Our ancestors must have been protecting you the entire way; let me give them each an incense to thank them," Li Nainai continued excitedly as she prepared incense to go to the place of worship.

"Nainai, there is something I must tell you," Xiao Si continued explaining.

"I heard from the other merchants that the Imperial Japanese army is coming. It was why they were eager to pay a higher price for your goods. They were afraid of not being able to stock up before the war breaks out."

Li Nainai tried to stay calm with this news.

"We, the Li family, have survived generations of occupations and wars. Absolutely nothing could kill us," Li

Nainai said with positivity.

She then ordered us to plant more corn as well as for Xiao Si to teach me how to dry the crops we grow so we could keep them longer.

"Our survival depends on it," Li Nainai said with a serious look on her face.

"We will budget some of the money from the crops to buy proper weapons to protect ourselves. We cannot rely on our country's army to protect our lives. They only know how to run for their lives as I recall," Xiao Si suggested to Li Nainai.

Li Nainai nodded in agreement, "We will need to be frugal with our spending."

Nainai brought all of us into the house of worship to pray to Li's ancestors. "Thank you for protecting our children Wuxiao, Kuaishou, and Xiao Si from any harm. Thank you for choosing for us a strong daughter-in-law, Kuaishou. Everyone else who traveled to the village with her has passed away except for her. I know you are all watching out for us," said Li Nainai as she bowed to thank the ancestors. "Please continue to keep our family safe and trouble free," Li Nainai repeated the prayers at least 10 times before we left the house of worship.

At the field, Wuxiao told the comrades about our trip to Taiyuan that the Imperial Japanese Army was attacking. Liye was upset by the news.

"Many think that Communists are associated with bandits!"

"Liye, those people are ignorant," replied Dong E.

"They were not wrong. A few of the comrades in Jiangxi felt upset about people suffering from starvation, including the bandits, and offered them food. A few bandits then joined our party in return. Chairman Mao was desperate to recruit as long as they followed the rules of our party. Of course, they were willing to follow any rules to keep from starving. Bandits are most likely to be unprincipled so, of course, we are not sure if they will continue following the rules. Who knows? Maybe they will also follow the Japanese Army's rules as well."

"Well, I think the most important thing is to protect our village from potential invasion? How can we keep all the comrades safe?" asked Wuxiao.

"I am not sure. I will need to send a letter to the authority of our party to figure out what to do in this scenario. I was used to only Guomindang who wanted to kill us. Now the Imperial Japanese Army is coming as well," replied Liye.

"Who is this Xiao Si person who saved all of your lives?" asked Dong E.

"Our servant," replied Wuxiao.

"We might need her to join the revolution as well. She would be a great person to have around," said Dong E.

Before dinner that evening, Wuxiao pulled Xiao Si aside and asked her to come to our party meetings. At first Xiao Si was reluctant, but after Wuxiao begged, she finally agreed.

"Can you keep it a secret from Nainai?" I asked Xiao Si.

"Of course, I don't want to get into trouble as well," promised Xiao Si.

Xiao Si arrived for the training with us the next day. She was surprised at the sight of Liye. Liye approached Xiao Si, "I thought the children were talking about you. But I thought it was another Xiao Si. Where have you been?"

"It was a long story, but Wuxiao's family saved me," replied Xiao Si.

Dong E turned to Wuxiao and me, "I can tell that they were lovers." We watched the interaction of Liye and Xiao Si and nodded.

"It looks like you have a lot to catch up on; we will leave you two alone. I can take the training from here," said Dong E loudly as she led the party to the next field so we could give Xiao Si and Liye distance.

A few weeks later, Liye received a letter from a Communist member instructing him to train us villagers to protect ourselves. From the evaluations Liye sent in, it was decided that comrade Guihua would be the leader of the Eight Route Army, and I was to be selected as the leader of the Children's Corp. The party also promised to get him some weapons so the village could potentially protect ourselves. Wuxiao congratulated me on being selected as the leader of Children's Corp. The members of the Chinese Communist Party had pitied me due to my early childhood experience. One day in the revolution training, Guihua gave me a nickname, "Kezai" which means to overcome misfortune. The party helped me to feel revitalized. With motivation to save our country and our home, I joined the Women's Association for Saving the Nation. I served alongside Dong E and learned how to sew shoes and clothing for the soldiers. We also learned the basics of human anatomy as well as how to remove bullets if a soldier needed to be saved.

I admired Dong E's patience and her beauty. From the gossip from our village, her relationship with her husband was seen as very admirable. They are both passionate about the Communist party. One day while sewing a uniform for the Eight Route Army, Dong E asked, "Aren't you a bit young to be a child bride?"

I nodded.

"How old were you?"

"About nine years old," I lied.

"Wow, I was married when I was 15. I was really lucky that it worked out this way. I cannot imagine being married at eight," she said, looking me up and down as if she was puzzled.

Time in the village had been passing by so fast. The daily farming routine and supporting activities with the Communist Party filled most of my time. I was already nine years old when the war broke out in Shanxi, but everyone else had thought I was thirteen. I was washing clothes one day at the river when news of the Battle of Taiyuan broke out. The other villagers at the river were worried about their relatives who had gone to Taiyuan as railroad workers.

"I heard they have been occupying Beijing since July. It was about time they came here for our resources," said a villager.

"Are you prepared? Better get some coal to cover up our faces and run south. I heard that the Japanese are ruthless."

The village was quieter than usual. It felt as if everyone was afraid of the battle happening at Taiyuan. One villager said, "If it can happen to Taiyuan, it can happen here to us." It was too close for comfort.

During dinner, Li Nainai was unusually quiet.

"The war is near us right now! What should we do?" asked Xiao Si that night during dinner.

"Did you prepare coal and weapons as I asked you to?" asked Li Nainai.

"Of course," replied Xiao Si.

"If the Japanese come here, please protect Wuxiao. He is still young. Don't worry about me," answered Li Nainai.

It seemed that no one in the village had any idea of what to do to prepare for the war. Everyone was solemn. Guihua asked us to be prepared.

"General Zhu De is in Taiyuan with Guomindang to fight this war. We should have nothing to worry about but, just in case, we should be prepared to help our comrades at the front line."

"Who is Zhu De?" asked Dong E.

"He is Mao's right hand man. In fact, they are the duo 'Zhu-Mao' which means pig's fur. He used to be a war lord and was addicted to opium. He wanted to join the

Communist party in the early days but was rejected. He then went to study abroad in Germany but was expelled for attending too many protests there. Then he studied in Russia and came back to China. Mao picked him because he understands western culture and is sophisticated, but yet has the heart of a peasant. He always has the brightest smile, as if everyone is okay, even during the roughest times. Everyone in the party thinks he is magical. I sure hope the sophisticated generals in Guomindang think so."

"Why is he helping Guomindang?" asked Liye.

"These are difficult times. Chairman Mao and Guomindang decided to work together as Chinese for once to fight the Imperial Japanese Army to save the civilians and our resources. If the Japanese take Shanxi, we will need to give up all of our resources for their army. Do you want that to happen?"

Liye was quiet. From their interactions, I started seeing why Guihua was selected to be the leader of the Eight Route Army in our village. Liye was like a set of fireworks—easily irritated and could be set off without thinking of any consequences. However, Guihua was careful, and looked at the whole picture instead of being reactive. He could remain level headed during the hardest of times, which is a quality that is hard to train.

As we were updated about the war, we began to fear more for our lives. Villagers started planning their escape routes in the mountains. A few of the wounded soldiers began escaping the war. One morning, in the field, we saw a group of them running into the village for help. The villagers were horrified by their bloody looks but many sympathized and offered help. As the soldiers recovered, they returned to the field—all but one. His name was Xi De. Because he was in the war, many villagers pitied him and offered him food. Xi De even shamelessly came to our training one day to beg for shelter and food.

"Winter is coming soon, it is cold at night. Can someone help me?"

"Shouldn't you be ashamed?" Liye asked him.

"I basically escaped death. I deserve some help."

Guihua and Liye looked at each other and shook their heads.

Guihua announced to our class that the front line needed help with drawing maps of the mountains. "Guomindang and the Imperial Japanese Army are no match for us because we know exactly where everything is. According to a letter from General Zhu De, the Guomindang has no idea how to fight the war. They only know how to send people to die in battle. The maps of the battles were inaccurate. If the war is coming closer, we need guerrilla fighters like us who know how to disguise ourselves in the wild and have accurate maps."

"I can help with this project," Xiao Si volunteered. A lot of other classmates also joined Xiao Si in surveying around the area to help with drawing the map.

"Also, we need some help in the rural area 15 lis away from Taiyuan to help remove bullets from our soldiers. The death count is rising, but we suspect, if there was help in the area such as helping soldiers with their wounds as well as removing bullets, we can save some soldiers to help save our county."

Dong E volunteered to go with protection of a few Eight Route Army soldiers. Her husband tried to stop her, "You will be captured!"

"Well, then do you want to come with?" Dong E asked him.

He agreed. They decided to leave the baby they recently had in the care of Dong E's Nainai.

"Your sacrifice for the country will never be forgotten," said Guihua to the couple as they left for the mission. It was as if he already knew the couple's fate.

Chapter 7

SNOW STARTED FALLING early this year and by early November, snow was piling up on the ground. The news of defeat in Taiyuan broke out in the village, creating a sense of despair.

"How did they lose? There were so many soldiers on our side!" asked Liye during our secret meeting sessions of the Chinese Communist Party.

"They lost the way we lost most wars. Guomindang troops just run for their lives as the army attacks. Even the Prince from Inner Mongolia fought better than the Guomindang," replied Guihua

"Wait, what do you mean? Was Inner Mongolia fighting on Japan's side?" asked Wuxiao.

"Yes, they are the Imperial Japanese's dogs now. Why are you surprised?" replied Guihua.

I felt lucky that I escaped Inner Mongolia. Their desperation must have influenced them to surrender. I started worrying about my family in my hometown. Are they okay?

"So what should we do now? Are the Japanese coming our way?" I asked Guihua.

"I am not sure. I have not heard from the leaders of our party for weeks."

His answer sent chills down my back. The room was silent.

During dinner that night, Li Nainai proposed that we lock up our food and hide our valuables throughout the house.

"Why?" asked Wuxiao.

"I can remember this from past disasters. Villagers usually start panicking. Then they will try to break in and steal our food. We need the crops we have been collecting throughout the months to keep our family alive," said Li Nainai.

Xiao Si followed Li Nainai's order and locked up the crops we had been saving.

As predicted, rumors spread that the Li family was the best fed in the village. Villagers at first started begging outside our front doors. As each one came to our door, Xiao Si had to cold heartedly reject them. I could see her sadness as she did so.

Eventually, the crowd outside our house grew.

"You heartless pig!" shouted one of the villagers.

"Our Li family does not owe you and we don't have any crops left," replied Xiao Si.

"You liar! Xi De told us that your family has food. You just want to starve all of us!" shouted another angry villager.

Xiao Si asked me how Xi De knew of this news.

"I have no idea," I lied.

The crowd eventually turned into a mob as passersby started joining the crowd. They started to become violent over the possibility of access to our food and began pushing. Xiao Si had no choice but to shoot at the leg of a villager.

"You witch!" the villager with the injured leg screamed.

The other villagers watched in terror as the injured villager was bleeding on the ground. The Eight Route Army got to our house just in time.

"Whoever tries to break into the Li family's house for anything will be shot to death!" shouted Liye. The villagers were frightened at this point and quickly dispersed.

Guihua got to the ground and offered help to the injured villager.

"Are you okay?" Liye asked Xiao Si.

Xiao Si nodded.

"That Xi De has been going around telling everyone that the Li family has enough food for the entire village. Is that true?"

Xiao Si refused to answer.

"Xi De must have heard our conversation in the field," said Wuxiao.

"I am not sure, but we cannot be talking about anything sensitive in public anymore. There are ears everywhere," I replied.

One day during spring time, Dong E's husband and a few of the Eight Route Army returned to the village, but Dong E was nowhere to be found.

"What happened to Dong E?" asked Guihua.

"We arrived at the station as ordered to help with the war. We were at the tent helping out and Dong E was removing soldiers' bullets at the tent. She left to get some fresh water for one of the soldiers and failed to return. We went looking for her and one of the villagers near the river told us that a Japanese soldier took her."

Dong E's husband looked extremely solemn.

"Well, let us find her," suggested Liye.

"I will come with," Guihua said.

"Are you sure? Don't you need to stay here in case of invasion?" Liye asked.

"A comrade is captured. You don't think that is important?"

"Can I also come with?" I asked. Liye and Guihua were surprised by my question.

"Well, she is my comrade too, so I guess we should all go and find her," I confirmed with the comrade.

Later that night while I was packing for the mission, Wuxiao and Xiao Si asked, "Are you sure you are going?"

"Yes. I need to find our comrade," I answered.

"Well, how can I explain to Li Nainai where you are," Xiao Si asked.

"Maybe I can also go, so I don't have to stay here and get into trouble," said Wuxiao.

"No way! If you go, Li Nainai will kill me even if we make it back alive," I told Wuxiao.

"Sorry, Xiao Si. Can you lie to Li Nainai and say that I went to the next village to help out an old woman?"

Xiao Is nodded, "I will see what I can do."

The soldiers and I traveled close to the frontline where there were more injured soldiers.

"Which river did she go to for water?" Guihua asked.

"Over there," pointed Dong E's husband.

We walked over to the river where Dong E was supposed to have been last seen. After carefully looking around, we found her shoe in the bushes next to the river.

"Are you looking for the owner of the shoe?" an older lady walked by and asked.

"Yes," Dong E's husband answered.

"A Japanese soldier took her. Poor girl. A few in our village are missing right now," the old lady continued.

"We have to find her. She could either be dead or be kidnapped," said Guihua.

That night, we headed north of the river to search for Dong E, but she was nowhere to be found. We saw a group of Japanese soldiers as we were trying to search.

"Let's hide to stay safe. There are too few of us here for a rescue mission," whispered Guihua.

Hiding in an abandoned hut, we heard a loud noise right outside. A group of Japanese soldiers were approaching the Eight Route Army and Guomindang's army. The Eight Route Army were fighting in guerrilla style as they scattered across the field. The point was to create confusion regarding positions from which they were attacking. We had practiced this many times but I never thought I would see it in a battle field.

"They must have extended the battle to this part of Shanxi already," whispered Guihua. I watched from our hiding spot. It was the bloodiest scene of my life.

Soldiers from the Eight Route Army were running around the hills and the hut. Most of them looked like peasants since our army could not afford the fancy uniforms and shiny boots of the Guomindang. The Eight Route Army wore only wearing black fabric shoes. Some of them were shot and wounded as many others bravely fought the battle that must have lasted for at least several hours.

"Should we join them?" I asked.

"Are you kidding? We don't even have weapons," answered Guihua.

Some time after the gunshots were over, we came out of the hut. Darkness was approaching and we saw dead bodies all across the hills. We were all silent as the wind blew on our faces.

"Good thing we were able to hide. This could have been us," said Dong E's husband.

Chapter 8

AFTER I RETURNED FROM our fruitless search for Dong E, I climbed the path to our home, where I knew Li Nainai awaited me with her wrath and her scornful derision. As my feet carried me up the steps, I could hear her voice pounding in my head, "Stupid girl! Insolent girl! The shame you bring us!" And so on.

My heart was heavy, anticipating the punishments that awaited me, but nothing dampened my spirits more than thinking about Dong E in the cold wilderness, a slave to the depredations of the Japanese invaders. What did they do to her? What would they do to all of us? While running back, my clothes were smeared with mud, dust and dead grass, I managed the final few steps and tried to catch my breath before opening the door, but I was not so fortunate. The moment I set foot underneath Li Nainai's eaves, the door was flung open and, in the shadow of the flickering coal fire inside, Nainai's silhouette stood out like a craggy, precipitous mountain.

"Get in this house right now," she said, her voice completely sullen and devoid of anger. She sounded tired and, as she held her arm out with a finger extended to the darkness within the home, I noticed how she trembled like a dead tree in a strong gale. Something was happening. The house was a flurry of activity; Xiao Si ran amok, back and forth across the sparsely decorated home, dragging luggage and piling it up near the door. Wuxiao stood solemnly in the corner, his head hanging low. He barely raised his eyes to meet my gaze and, despite my best efforts to retain my pride, the menacing glare of Nainai cut through me, and I felt my heart begin to flutter.

Not now, I urged myself. *Keep it together.*

"Do you realize what is happening? Do you realize how much you have nearly cost this family? The Japanese are marching around the province, taking what they can and burning the rest. Word has gotten around that they are raping all the women. You don't want to be in either category. You don't want to be anywhere near them."

I could tell she was speaking sincerely and, for the first time in the many years I had spent as a guest in her house, I began to feel sympathy for the old crone. She wanted only to hang onto what she knew and, with every passing day, her tenuous grasp slipped a little bit more. Age was bearing down on her and war was no place for the infirm.

"Li Nainai, I only wanted to help our people..."

"Help your people? We are your people. I am your people! I have been feeding you all these years!"

I glanced briefly over at Wuxiao, hoping for support, but my husband kept his gaze trained at the floor as if, by standing mute and still, he was hoping that his grandmother would forget about his presence entirely. Xiang Si continued to run about, gathering supplies for what looked to be a long journey and, after trekking through the ashen battlegrounds after the fight, I had no resistance left in me. I looked at the pile of luggage—useless trappings of the old way that Li Nainai would never be able to live without—and felt a pang of mourning for her, for her customs, for her way of thinking. It was all over now. One way or another.

As Li Nainai continued to berate me, I shuffled my weight from one side to the other and waited for it to be over. Xiao Si burst forth from the courtyard, the door to the outside stables banging against the wall and shaking the decorations hanging there. A cold wind followed her like a bad omen, chilling me through my sopping clothing. "They are coming!" she shouted. Her voice was laden with sincere fear, and the pitch to which her voice rose set my own fingers jittering as I strove to remain calm. As if the frantic shouting of Xiao Si—usually so serene and calm—shook something loose in the old woman's heart, she began to bark orders at the three of us, appearing for a brief moment to be the powerful matriarch that she once was.

"Xiao Si, load up the donkey; grab everything you can! Kuaishou, get my travelling attire ready. Wuxiao, grab as much grain as you can carry, as many beans as possible, all of the corn!"

Xiao Si sprung into action, with Wuxiao running out behind her, each enthralled by the terror of the Japanese that sat firmly in the center of every Chinese heart. My heart pounded, but I did not move.

"Li Nainai," I began, my voice calm. "We cannot bring these trunks. They are too heavy and the donkey cannot hold it all. We must leave now and travel light if we are to escape."

Li Nainai stared at me with a cold, unyielding gaze. She whispered so low that I strained to hear her over the rising wind that tore through the village, shaking branches and sending paper lanterns bouncing down the hillsides.

"As long as I live, you are mine. Don't you forget that. I have seen this family through worse than war. Do what I say!" I had never seen Li Nainai filled with rage and anxiety in the time I had spent here.

"There is no time!" I protested, and I had a list of reasons ready why we did not have the travelling capacity for her luxury items, but my tirade was cut short by the crack of flesh on flesh as she drew back her hand and slapped me across my cheek with the bony backside. I never would have imagined such a tiny old woman had such power in her, and I stared in dumbfounded awe at the trembling, angry mess she had become. Without hesitation, I began carting her trunks outside and hoisting them on top of the cart, feeling terrible for our donkey with every box. He stared impassively at the ground in front of him, not dissimilar from Wuxiao's stance in the house.

Xiao Si, Li Nainai, Wuxiao, and I joined the herd of villagers crowding the mountain paths, congregating on the main road that led down the mountain, shuffling with confusion. We did not know where to go. The empty, vacant looks on the elderly farmers' faces made me think that the entire village shared our problem. The rains came and, before long, the narrow road leading to the southwest became a muddy river that we all stumbled over, slipping and struggling to retain our footing. The icy wind rolled down from the snowy passes overhead, chilling everyone. Mothers cradled babies tightly against their chest, bunched up their clothing for warmth, and begged for assistance. No one stopped to help. We kept walking.

We fell behind quickly. Our donkey—laden with supplies and vanity objects of Li Nainai—earned us derisive and jealous stares from the people around us. The donkey struggled to bear the load and the three of us carried as much as our small frames would allow. My feet ached, and I hated the practice of foot binding more than I had ever hated anything in my life. Every step was agony and Li Nainai's refusal to get down from the cart and help us carry the load made my blood boil with rage. I tried to ignore my feelings. The anger surging within me served only to sap my energy and I had none to spare for this grueling trek.

Before long, the other families spread out on the road, and we were left on our own. They were probably glad to see Li Nainai falling behind and left her intentionally to slow down the Japanese when they finally caught up. The four of us shared no words, had no conversation. We only kept our heads down and continued to march through the freezing rain that was quickly becoming snow now that the weather had gotten colder. Despair arrived on the morning of the third day when we rose from our mats underneath the cart, huddled together for warmth against the cold night winds. The donkey was not breathing. His eyes had the same peaceful look that they always had, as if he did not mind his fate. Looking around at the desolate and windswept valley that we found ourselves in, I wished to join him.

"Li Nainai," said Wuxiao, "We must move quickly. The Japanese will catch us any day."

Xiao Si and I both agreed, eager to convince the elder matriarch that the Japanese were bearing down on us, that they would show no mercy to an elderly woman and three children. That they hated us as much as we hated them, and that neither side would give up the fighting until the other was dead and buried. But she would not be dissuaded. The trunks and the luggage, the baggage that the three of them dragged behind in the mud—this was everything that Li Nainai had ever known—family heirlooms, tokens of remembrance for ancestors long gone. None of it mattered to me. I cared only about getting off the mountain before the Japanese found us wriggling like dying fish in the mud.

"These trunks are our history, our legacy," she would say, her haughty demeanor completely unaffected by the mud caking her thighs and smearing her stately apparel. "If we leave our history behind, then what are we?"

Alive and smart, I wanted to say, but I held my tongue. I held my tongue like I held it throughout the years of living with the Li family. After all, my family sold me to strangers. What did I care about the legacies and histories of someone else's family? It was all going to be washed away by the war anyway. Wuxiao pleaded endlessly with her until she finally gave in. With a great, exasperated sigh, she threw her arms in the air and said, "After so much, this is the worst moment of my life. My ancestors will follow me with curses." But she ceded. They left the baggage and the trunks in a neatly stacked pile on the side of the road. With a heavy heart, they continued walking; Li Nainai continued to complain as the rains continued and darkness set in on the third day.

The next morning, Wuxiao and Xiao Si went ahead to scout the area, to see if the Japanese could be seen or if they could find any signs of safety in the distance. They left me alone with Li Nainai, who sat and grumbled by the dying embers of our twig fire.

"We must put that out, Nainai," I said, trying to keep the edge out of my voice. "They will see the smoke."

But Li Nainai said nothing and only continued to rock back and forth on the balls of her feet.

"Nainai. Please. We must get ready to march."

"Leave me here." The words came in a short, quiet burst, as if the very speaking of them hurt the old woman's soul. Looking at her in the growing light of the morning, I realized how truly ancient she was. The sagging flesh that dropped around her eyes gave her face the appearance of a gnarled tree trunk, and her wispy white hair looked frazzled, like clouds scattered by a strong wind.

"I cannot, Nainai. You are one of us. We need to leave here together."

"We aren't related. You are a curse."

I had expected this and the words meant nothing to me. What did sting me, what set my heart trembling and my lips quivering, was the malice that hung off every syllable, as if I had personally induced the Japanese soldiers to invade our province and kill our villagers. As if I were the one kidnapping little girls and selling them for money.

"I won't hear it, Nainai. I—", my words were stopped by two hulking figures that loomed at the edge of our meager campsite. They held bayonets, pointed directly at us, and the gaping maw of those tools of death looked wide enough to swallow an entire chicken. Japanese. So they had found us. As I watched the last tendrils of smoke drifting away in the breeze, I cursed myself for giving into Nainai. I cursed myself for not fighting with the Eighth Road Army like I should have been doing. Better to die in battle than let these two men seize me.

Immediately after I noticed the two, they began screaming in some barbaric language that made no sense to my ears. I did not know any Japanese at all, and the guttural syllables they barked at us seemed to come from a deep crack in the mountainside, where demons waited to ensnare unwitting travelers. Nainai tried to jump up, but the soldiers fell upon her with the butts of their rifles and, when I jumped into the fray, they threw me aside like a sack of potatoes, sending me toppling to the ground. My dress flew up and my shame was revealed to everyone. The soldiers—two at first, but now too many to count—surrounded us and laughed as my Nainai pleaded with them in Mandarin to stop their pillage. They continued to laugh and slapped Nainai so hard she fell to the ground beside me and said no more.

To my horror, one of the men—he seemed to be in charge and his uniform was so much better kept than those around him—stepped up to me, bent to the ground, and picked up a tiny pamphlet that had fallen from my waist band. He looked at me, looked at the pamphlet, then back at me. I don't know what he said, but after he barked a command at his soldiers, they stood over me and Nainai, took their rifles, and began clubbing us. I shouted for them to stop as the blood ran from Nainai's head,

"You'll kill her!" I shouted, but they wouldn't let up. Finally, they landed one more blow to my own head, and I felt the sticky warmth running down my cheeks and tasted the copper flavor in my mouth before the hazy, foggy morning swallowed up everything, and left me in a void of unconsciousness.

Chapter 9

I WOKE UP IN THE VILLAGE of Jingui located at the top of a mountain, where the wind did not let up for one second, and its unyielding wail all around us sounded like the wailing of Nainai when the Japanese fell upon us. Nainai. What had happened to her? Where was she? Did they take her to this lonely mountain top or worse? I suddenly had a horrid image flash across my mind: Nainai, with the fear of death and dishonor still wrought upon her usually serene features, laying in a pool of her own frozen blood at the bottom of a steep incline, her limbs twisted and bent out of shape, her skin, pale.

Questions raged in my head with the same relentless battering of the wind against the rocky outcropping, slowly chipping away. Of course, I had no answers. I did not know where I was, let alone where they had taken my mother-in-law. I didn't know how much time had passed, what had become of Xiao Si and my husband or anything. All I knew was that the Japanese had taken us and that now

I sat with my back to the damp cold of a smooth rock, that the food they gave me had less nutrition than the maggots squirming and tunneling through it, and that I might never see any of my adopted family members again. These thoughts produced in me a melancholy that would not abate and, every time my captors opened the rickety wooden door of the hovel they kept me in, I had to fight with every bit of willpower I could muster not to throw myself at their feet and plead for mercy. To grovel. To wrap my arms around their muddy boots and cry until they kicked me off with a dismissive gesture. I wanted to every time but never did. I sat impassively as the guards taunted me, barking at me with their guttural and bizarre sounding language that made me think of ravenous dogs in the starving valleys during famine years. The only light that was afforded to me was the slim sliver that slipped in through the warped wooden door, which was only enough to drive me mad with a crushing awareness of the passing days.

One day, a man came into my hovel and squatted on his haunches, silent, not saying anything. His cleanly pressed uniform and the impeccable polish of his black leather boots made me think he was important, and the austere severity of his words as he spoke grammatically perfect Mandarin confirmed what I suspected. Only officers were smart enough to master our language. For a long time, he said nothing and we locked eyes. I knew I recognized him, but I could not remember if I had seen him in the battle when I was searching for Dong E or if he was with the men who kidnapped me and my Nainai.

"You can use a bath, I presume," he said, affecting the kind manner of an uncle who rarely gets to visit. Despite the seething hatred I felt inside me, I felt my wrath subside a little as he turned his warm smile to me. "Perhaps a cigarette, if you are old enough?"

"I'm old enough." I didn't know where this was going and I didn't want a cigarette, but I definitely did not want this Japanese dog mocking me. He reached into his pocket, pulled out a fresh paper wrapping with crisp, fragrant cigarettes inside. He fished one out, put it to his lips and pulled out a lighter. He hesitated for a moment, looking at me with his inquisitive stare and then lit up. The smoke filled the room with a pungent aroma that made me think of food even as it stung my eyes, and I was assailed by the ludicrous notion that, if given the chance, I would gladly eat every fiber of tobacco in the entire pack and smile afterward. I had never known such hunger as I now experienced.

But rather than offer me a cigarette, he reached behind his back, and removed from his waistband a familiar, wrinkled and water stained document—a small pamphlet with faded red leather covering tattered pages. My manual, given to me by Dong E. I tried not to let my surprise and anger show when he flipped through the pages of my book. His audacity was limitless, to be irreverently flipping through the pages like that, smiling, billowing clouds of smoke in my direction. "Perhaps you would like to explain how you ended up with this, and then I may find it in my heart to give you a cigarette. Or an apricot. Whatever you like."

He smiled at me again, but I saw no familial affection in his eyes. He looked like a hungry wolf. The man from the mountain pass. The leader of the soldiers who took me and Nainai. The revelation produced a sinking feeling in the pit of my stomach and I felt suddenly that I would vomit—despite my extreme hunger—on his shoes if he did not move away from me.

I said nothing. I *could* say nothing.

"Child, you do know that we are at war with the Eighth Road Army and their dogged philosophies, their childish ideas. Having this book is very serious trouble for you and yours. We have good information from one of your former comrades that your travelling party was involved with the criminals in this gang." He threw the book into a sopping puddle that had collected in an imprint of the rock floor. I watched with anguish as the pages soaked up the slimy water. In the silence, the wind continued to howl outside, and the gray-white sky visible through the open door of the hut promised early snowfall in the high mountains. It would be a cold winter, I realized in a distant, disconnected way, the words reaching my consciousness like an overheard statement from the other side of a wide, slow moving river.

"Perhaps you can tell me how you ended up carrying such a rag?"

"I found it." The words came out quick and quiet and I regretted them the moment I heard their reverberation against the rock walls that surrounded us.

"Found it?" He shrugged his shoulders. "I see that you found it, and am only curious about where that might have been."

"I swear. I cannot even read."

"And what is a girl who cannot read doing finding and storing dangerous communist ideas?"

"I—"

Before I could throw out any more excuses, the man stood up and, as his shadow fell on me, his incredible height and the wide stature of his frame made me feel like a child again, tugging at my father's clothing while he sat listless in the thrall of opium smoke that emanated constantly from his nose and lips. He drew back his hand with a sharp inhale and brought the backside of his bony hand down against my cheekbones, sending me sprawling into the same puddle that had consumed my pamphlet. It felt as if he had stabbed my face with a hot poker and tears welled up in my eyes. Rather than show him my pain, I kept my face against the cool surface of the dust and grit and mud below me, trying to hold back my fear.

"You still do not know the name of the person who gave that book to you?"

"I swear—"

He slapped me again and kicked me in the ribs as I tried to scuttle away from him. At that moment, I thought I would never draw breath again. I tried to gasp, but nothing would enter my lungs. I gulped and clutched at my throat and turned to the man with my tear stained, fearful eyes, but he continued to look at me as if I were a dog in the road eating his chickens.

"Take her to the tree," he said, his voice returning to the same state of calm with which he first addressed me.

As the men standing outside my hovel stomped into the tight enclave, I tried to push myself back against the wall, to recede from them as much as I possibly could in some vain and outlandish hope that they would not see me if I made myself really small. I closed my eyes tight, and the feeling of their slender fingers strangling my wrists and yanking me to my feet was like the talons of a hawk coming to scoop up a baby child.

The soldiers marched me barefoot down the rocky path that I had climbed—how long ago? Jagged stone pricked and sliced into the bottoms of my feet with every step and, despite my best attempts at keeping my posture erect and my head up, the painful incisions digging into my not-totally-healed bound up feet forced me to walk with the shameful hunch of a common criminal slinking to the gallows. The wind rising from the valley below sent the rags that barely clung to my body fluttering as I shivered, trying to bunch my arms up into my torso as best as the restraints would allow. Still, I scanned the scene before me. Japanese soldiers stood with disinterested looks on their monotonous faces, watching with only the mildest curiosity as I walked by. Above, the village of Jingui had been turned into a fortress, with all of the sparse trees in the area being converted into menacing posts and boards for the wall that now enclosed what could only be a Japanese encampment. Guards patrolled atop the wall above, and a light snow had just begun to fall. A hawk soared, circling the area, and I imagined her looking down at me with the same sense of boredom that the war weary Japanese had upon their faces. Beige patches of bristly dead grass stuck up from rock crags here and there, and that was the only vegetation remaining. Everything else had been harvested or had already dried up and died. Except for the tree. A locust.

With its limbs stripped bare, it had a menacing appearance, and its limbs reaching up to the clouds seemed to engulf the village and the mountaintop it was perched upon. At that moment, I did not think I had ever seen a bigger tree. It loomed in the distance, and my feeling of dread grew with every step as it loomed larger and larger with each step.

The leader continued his conniving questions throughout the journey, but I paid him no attention and did not, for one instant, take my gaze away from the tree. As I drew closer, I could see that its bark had been stripped away at the base of its trunk and that the normally white wood inside was stained a delicate pink color. Snow began to stick to its sides, and the man's voice was swallowed up by a brisk gust of wind.

"—very easy for yourself," came the man's voice after the wind had died down. "There is no need for you to suffer, if you can just point us to the houses of the men who are printing that garbage."

When we came to a halt before the tree, I had to crane my neck upward to gaze at its extremities and the motion made my head spin from exhaustion and hunger. Before I had a chance to react or take a single breath, the hawkish claws of my captors locked around my wrists again and, with limp legs dragging behind me, I was brought up against the tree, spun around, and bound to its cold, frozen surface with my hands high above my head. The areas where a few patches of persistent bark clung for life to the tree trunk scraped against my flesh and reminded me that I was not dreaming. They tied the rope tightly on my wrists and hung me on the tree. My feet were far from the ground.

Even through the pall of cloud cover that smothered the valley, the sunlight blinded me after so many hours— days?—spent in the hovel. I could scarcely open my eyes and had no idea that the man who smoked his cigarettes and paraded around in his perfectly presentable boots was being armed by his men with a bamboo switch. I heard his footsteps as he clomped up to me, the frozen ground below him crunching as he drew closer. When he stopped before me, I felt his hot breath against my neck, and I opened my eyes to stare into his own, just centimeters away from my face. The clear hatred encased there shook my spine and made my stomach turn for the third time that morning. He grabbed my rotting clothing—a burlap sack with three holes torn into it and nothing more—and yanked them away from me. I felt the frigid air wash over my naked torso and chest like cold surf swallowing up a drowning sailor, but the mountain air was nothing compared to the intense heat of my shame, welling up from my bosom and bringing color to my cheeks.

"Where did you get the book?" he shouted, the words echoing in the mountain air before being carried off by the wind. Before I had the chance to stammer a response, I felt the white hot explosion of pain searing my ribs. I tried to flinch away but the ropes offered no give, no range of movement at all. He asked the same question again and again while beating me with a bamboo stick. I could barely hear him as my mind was focused on the pain from the beating. The rope had cut into my wrist as I was flinching, trying to escape this. Blood started running from my wrist and dripped onto my thighs. I screamed in agony, caring no longer about shame or propriety. Only about the intense, animalistic feeling of terror that the man's bamboo had brought me.

I do not know how long this persisted, but I felt like I had aged significantly when it was done. I cried, ushering forth the laments of a broken woman. I knew how pathetic I sounded. I knew that the Japanese were sniggering behind their cupped hands and were planning on doing who knew what afterward. But I did not care. I wailed and wailed, trying to meet the rising tide of wind scouring over the rocky path. I screamed until my throat felt like I had swallowed gravel and I could no longer recognize the sounds coming from my mouth. They released me from the tree and, as I felt a sense of relief, the man that was interrogating me got on top of me, took off his belt with excitement. There, he forced himself into me. I screamed in terror. After he was finished, he waved his hand at the other soldiers who were guarding the stronghold to take their turns. I closed my eyes and passed out in exhaustion and pain.

Chapter 10

AFTER MY ORDEAL ON THE locust tree, the Japanese soldiers brought me to a new cell—a hole in the craggy rocks of the mountaintop outfitted with a wooden door held together by iron braces, and a thin, rotting mat of sorghum stalks that scratched at my fresh wounds and kept me in a constant state of agony throughout my time in that crypt of a hovel. I shared this tiny space with one other girl, Xinyi Sung. In the day time, soldiers came in as if we were animals or some objects to satisfy their sexual hunger. The soldiers came in during the day time, tortured and robbed us of our youth and innocence. At night, when bad weather filled the valley with squalls and snowfall, we would huddle together in the corner farthest from the door, grabbing at each other and squeezing each other's sinuous muscles for warmth, security, and comfort as we ate the rations brought to us by the Japanese.

I do not know how many days have passed. I had ceased counting a while ago and, though Xinyi Sung busied herself scratching markers into the rock walls that closed us in every time the Japanese brought us rations, I stared at the wall, watching it fill up with tiny white slash marks. But I never counted them. I didn't want to know. I wanted to know about Nainai and Wuxiao.

Xinyi Sung—her matted hair and animalistic dispositions betraying how long she had been a prisoner—first approached me on a cold night with snow blasting its way through the cracks of our door and peppering us with ice crystals. She whispered in my ear.

"Kuaishou."

I was drifting off and, for an ephemeral moment, it felt as if I may have heard my name uttered in a dream. It sounded so much like my old friend Meiling, whom I had not thought of in so many years.

"Kauishou, wake up!"

The whispers came with the menace of a cobra announcing its presence and my illusions were shattered. I knew exactly who spoke my name with such a conspiratorial whisper in the dead of night.

"Would you be with me if I told you I had a plan?"

I considered my answer for a moment and also considered pretending to be as fast asleep, huddled up on the rotting sorghum. But Xinyi pressed: "I know you're not asleep. You talk in your sleep."

"What plan can you possibly have?"

"One that will work."

I raised my voice in surprise but the girl cut me off with a harsh hissing sound: "*Quiet!* Or they'll hear you.

We can get out of here. There are five of us and never more than two guards. Each guard has two guns and one knife. My guess is that we are on the western side of their base. The slope of the mountain is rigorous and full of peril, but I know the way. If we made a break, they might get one or two of us but not all."

The words sounded like lunacy, and the only thing that proved I was actually hearing them—not dreaming them—was the bitter cold that sank its teeth into my toes every time Xinyi Sung shifted their weight.

"We have not eaten in days," I said. "Only gruel. Those soldiers are trained and fed."

"Trained, maybe. But not fed. Besides, if you are here, you must have been trained as a guerrilla fighter. We all were."

I thought back to my time with the Eighth Road Army in Wuxiao's village, where I attended the lectures and listened to Dong E explaining the easiest way to kill a Japanese or a nationalist with readily available house-hold objects. I missed her and, despite my best hopes, I had very little faith that she was still alive. What did she teach me? What about those childish seminars prepared me for the circumstances I now faced?

Xinyi Sung was like a feral animal by this point, a caged dog desperate for freedom. She would say anything. Do anything.

"I know you are thinking about the locust tree. Believe me, so am I. But if the Japanese decide to move out of this mountain village, they may decide that it is too much trouble to bring a bunch of slave girls. We are disposable."

"I will think about it, Xinyi, but I don't think it is a good move."

"I didn't think you would say that. I thought I recognized... something in you. A spirit."

I said nothing but, in the darkness, I heard the rustling and scraping sounds of Xinyi struggling to find some warmth in the barren cell, curling up tight against the sorghum mat, my own body, and the damp rocks. Her words echoed through my head and, though I stood very little chance of actually escaping, I wanted to escape.

I awoke the next morning to a brilliant splash of sunlight falling on our huddled bodies, warming my cheeks and reminding me briefly of the cold winter mornings that I had enjoyed with my father—before his crippling opium addiction had taken him from me. The illusion did not last. Immediately, the already cramped cave was filled with Japanese soldiers who piled in and leveled rifles at us and, when Xinyi Sung awoke to the gaping muzzles staring back at us, a panic ensued. We tried to squirm our way into the back, trying to avoid the hail of bullets that would surely come for us at any moment.

I gave up. I did not squirm or fidget, but rather stared back impassively at the Japanese dogs who had the face of children—rosy cheeks and wet, reflective eyes. Then, the commandant entered, and he was so tall that he had to stoop his shoulders to fit into the room. His presence filled the cave, and it suddenly felt as if the hole in the ground did not contain enough breathable air for everyone occupying it.

"Stand them up, strip them," he said, as if he were telling his butchers how to prepare a pork roast. The soldiers immediately responded to his orders and, while the last vestiges of sleep were torn from my eyes, the soldiers fell on my rags, tearing them from my body and again exposing my shame to all present. Only the solidarity of Xinyi—also naked and trembling as the cold wind billowed through the cave—prevented my cheeks from flushing with hot blood. Xinyi's body was filled with more red marks and dried blood than my own body. I was wondering what had happened to her body.

The commandant regarded us closely, staring at every centimeter or our bodies with his hands clasped behind his back and his brow ruffled by thought.

"Raise your arms," he said to Xinyi, and she did.

"Stand on your toes," he said and, though she was trembling with fear and emotional exhaustion, Xinyi obeyed his command. He looked at each of us as if he would not forget the slightest detail, as if he were cataloguing every blemish, every imperfection that our bodies had to offer.

I hated him and the hatred burned in my eyes when he halted before me. His fingers caressed my breasts and sent chills down my spine. He cupped them, squeezed firmly, and he smiled at my revulsion. His calloused fingers were rough and scratched at the tender skin underneath my bosom. His teeth were rotting, and his breath smelt like he had been away in the jungle valleys below for some time. Without breaking eye contact, he spoke to his men in Mandarin, making sure that I understood what he was saying: "She'll do."

All at once, the soldiers fell upon me. I tried to fight, desperately hoping that Xinyi Sung would come to my aid but, of course, it was impossible. What could she do? One girl against a band of Japanese dogs? They threw a sack over my head and I was again cast in darkness, unaware of the direction in which they hauled me off.

Through the sacking cloth, I could feel the day's warmth and sunshine, despite the early winter setting in. In better times it would have brought a smile to my face. I always loved a warm day at the end of fall, right before the impossibly cold grips of winter took hold of the valley. But I was given no time to enjoy the warmth, even if I had been capable of doing so at the time. They marched uphill at full speed and I knew at once they were bringing me into the fortress.

I smelled camp fires smoking in the crisp air and, despite my fear, my mouth watered at the succulent fragrance of pork brazing in a great, big cast iron pot. I heard the barking laughter of soldiers, the creaking hinges of the great wooden gate they had built around the village center when they occupied the mountain. I heard the cries of an old man though, with the sacking cloth over my head, I had no notion of what beset him. His cries were accompanied by the crash of a box smashing on the rocky ground and the laughter of Japanese soldiers redoubled with great vigor. Finally, I heard the deafening and portentous slam as the gate closed behind me, shaking snowfall from its eaves.

I was then led into a warm building with hard wooden floors that felt so smooth and wonderful beneath my scarred and calloused feet. Eventually, we came to a stop, I was forced to my knees and the bag was removed. I kneeled in the center, naked, and struggling to shield my bosom from the licentious eyes of a ring of Japanese soldiers. They looked no older than Dong E, but, by the prim and arrogant arrangement of their lapels and medals and perfectly creased pants, I figured they were officers. They stared at me with smiles plastered to their faces and hollow eyes that had nothing left in them. The commandant said "You all are here because you led your men with bravery and you all killed many Chinese. She is for you."

He turned and walked out of the room with his signature marshal stride, his air of dignity and respectability following in his wake. In his absence, the Japanese—who were already something less than human—became worse even than the many dogs that come out of the forests as winter settles in. Their clammy hands grabbed at every inch of my flesh as they threw me to the ground. My chin slammed the cement floor, but the pain did not even register as blood trickled from the freshly opened wound there. I tried to kick back against them, like an agitated donkey bucking its load but, within seconds, their hands were squeezing my arms, pinning down my shoulders, wrapping themselves around my neck, and tightening their grips. In the fury of the moment, their faces blended into each other and I made no differentiation between them.

Dogs, one and all. I felt them everywhere, like they were one insidious being, a demon from the same hell. Their fingers traced delicate patterns inside my thighs and I landed a kick into one man's groin that sent him sprawling back into the waiting arms of his comrades. They laughed. Even he laughed as he gripped his testicles and groaned in pain. It was a joke to them and, at that moment, I faced the horror of what was coming. I cried out against them as they kicked me and beat me into submission, each and every blow standing out in my mind as pain flared up first through my ribs, then from my thighs, then my arms. Then the pain blended together into one infernal sensation that swallowed up my body.

All at once, the grabbing and the touching grew more intense and, though I did not speak their language, I knew by the aggression in their voices that they were fighting over me. Over who would go first. "Help!" I screamed. I had never heard such panic in my voice, and the thought of the Japanese affecting me so caused my face to flush with even greater shame than the beating they were bestowing upon me. One man strode up to where I lay on the floor and slapped me hard in the face with the back of his hand. I felt warm blood pooling in my mouth and it spilled onto the floor when he pushed my face into the cement below me. With my gaze riveted to the wall before me, I heard the individual voices squabbling just as surely as I felt their fingers going everywhere, anywhere. Like worms digging through a rotting carcass. I wanted to cry. I wanted to scream. I wanted to rage against them and sink my teeth into one of their throats and refuse to let go until they had no choice but to shoot me dead right there. Mostly, however, I wanted to be back in the village.

Tears welled up in my eyes, and they spilled over when I felt the cold pain of their penetration, their awkward and arrhythmical thrusting going all the way up into my belly. With each thrust, I felt like a railroad spike had been driven into my womb and I shrieked every time despite my resolve to silently bear their assaults. It felt like being stabbed. Countless times. Though I had vowed not to scream in front of these demons, they refused to let up, and as the minutes crawled by like hours, they increased their paces, their aggression. Pushing my body up against the wall until my nose was flat against it and my laments were muffled by its hard surface. Pulling back against my hair, slapping me, spitting at me moaning, crying, groaning, scratching, biting, kicking.

I tried. With every bit of strength I had left in me—which, considering the food I had been eating, was not much—I tried to fight back against them. I flailed my limbs and felt a grim, animal satisfaction when my nails sliced into the flesh of the second man to rape me. He fell back, still laughing, as another took his place. Again, the thrusting. Again, the stabbing.

Again, the humiliation and the pain and the tears and the fighting back, but nothing would stop them. I was lost then and I knew that nothing in my life would ever repair itself. I thought about Wuxiao and the indignity he would feel if he knew that his wife was penetrated by Japanese dogs. I thought about the comments from Nainai. Their faces surfaced through my terror and my pain, one by one, until I felt the shame of everyone in my life knowing about this and judging, wagging fingers, whispering behind cupped hands. This would end me. I would die, and if I didn't, I would wish that I had.

Every humiliation and horror was acted out upon me until I went limp and the cries began to burst forth from my lungs. I lost control. The pain of their rape was nothing to the humiliation and, as I felt warm blood trickling down my inner thighs, I went blank. As the beatings and the penetration went on and on, it became monotonous. I convinced myself I was bored even though I felt the worst embarrassment I had ever experienced. They cheered for one another.

And they laughed. And they continued.

I don't know exactly how long it went on, but I know that when they marched me out of the cave, the sun had been poking out behind the eastern mountains, and now, as they brought me back to the cell—marching me still naked and covered in their saliva and everything else that I did not want to think of—the sun had peaked in the sky and was beginning its descent toward the deserts of the west.

Xinyi was horrified at my condition, but I felt as if she was really horrified that it would happen to her before we got off this rock. I did not care for her sympathies and flinched away from her touch. That night, though, as she drifted off to sleep, I turned to Xinyi, shook her awake, and whispered in her ear "It's time."

Before that moment, I never once got the impression of affection from that cold and determined woman and, in the all years between then and now, I have not experienced her warmth again. But after I rolled away from her that night, I felt a small hand reach out from the pile of girls cowering from the cold in the cave and caress my own. I did not need to look over toward her to know that the hand was hers.

Chapter 11

I WOKE UP THE NEXT MORNING with my joints aching and my flesh bruised. Every movement caused an explosion of pain that seemed to encompass every centimeter of my body and my head pounded with a steady rhythm that was exacerbated by the sunlight that intruded on my discomforting dreams. Slowly, the memories came back, though only in flashes. The cold rock of my cell reminded me of the hardwood floor and the abrasions that were scattered across my chin and cheeks and forehead, stung with the salty lime buildup on their rough surfaces.

When Xinyi reached over to touch me, to probe me awake and to offer her condolences, I flinched away from her, remembering only the sickening grace with which the Japanese soldiers had caressed me. The pleasurable tickle of their infernal fingers haunted me and my stomach felt awfully sick. "I am sorry," she said, barely a whisper. A timid sound that was swallowed up the rigid surfaces of the hollow rock they had thrown us in. "What to say..." I made no reply, at first, but soon I turned over toward her, wincing with the effort as the bruises on my hips ground themselves against the sorghum mat. "We have to start planning. We have... to be... ready."

Even speaking the words stung, as if I had a broken rib jutting out of my lungs, and every inhalation drove the ragged edges of the wound further apart. She stared at me with a solemn but severe gaze and only nodded in response—a tiny gesture, barely discernible. But the fierce determination of her gaze, coupled with the subtle, lurking terror that hid just below the surface, communicated her response well enough. At any moment, the opportunity might present itself, and we would have to remain alert.

For a while, after our brief conversation, we sat in silence, neither one addressing the other. The still, stagnant air of the cell almost gave the moment a sense of serenity, but the momentary peace was shattered by the slamming of the door as it bounced against the stone surface behind. Instantly, our cell was filled with guns and soldiers once more. We pleaded for mercy, falling to our knees and scarcely managing to hold in our shrill shrieks of terror when the Commandant entered. He made an attempt at surveying us, no formality of stripping us naked and playing with our breasts and making us complete inane tasks. He only looked absently at the soldier to his right, and said, "Take them." And then they took us. Bags over our heads, ropes on our wrists. A forced march up the hill and into the gates of the fortress that loomed over the surrounding villagers' homes. My feet and knees and arms ached, and the bouncing of my head from side to side as I struggled to keep up with the soldiers made me dizzy. I felt my stomach turning over as I thought about going through it again, about their fingers groping at every crack and crevice of my body, and for the first time since my ordeal had begun, I felt grateful for the cloth that they had thrown over my head. I would have hated for them to see my trembling, nervous fear.

They brought the two of us to the same building in which I had been raped the previous day and removed the sacks from our heads. Light flooded in. The Japanese officers milling about the headquarters looked at us and at one another with a thinly veiled and ravenous hunger that made my bruises seem to swell, and a throbbing pain emanate from my heart and out toward the extremities of my frame. I looked into every eye through the swollen cheek bones they had left me with but I could not make out any familiar faces. I wanted to see them, the men who raped me. I wanted to know the shame that would be in their eyes, even though I knew with equal surety that such shame would be completely absent from the Japanese dogs. They knew nothing about it.

As we snaked through the narrow corridors of the building that must have served the villagers as a town forum in more pleasant days, I did, however, see other faces that I knew. Women, girls. Children. They all had the same bruises up and down their sturdy faces, the same looks of resolve. Some wore flowing, beautiful robes that trailed behind them and had their faces painted in the ugly manner of the Japanese whore, looking like a child's doll, and I could see even beneath all of that face paint that they burned with shame and hatred and the thousand conflicting emotions of a hostage at war. I scanned the faces for anyone that I may have known, anyone from the Eighth Route Army or from Wuxiao's village. I did not see anyone, though I did see the familiar look in every face. The look that pleaded for help, though it knew that help would not come. All of the women had that look, though none of them looked broken yet.

When Xinyi Sung and I were marched into a room adjacent to the room I had been led to the day before, the guards who kept firm grasps on our elbows pushed us forward. With our wrists still behind our backs, we slammed into the floor with a resonating thud. The soldiers formed a ring around us, and the two of us pressed against each other, the warmth of each other's backs soothing in the cold morning air that filtered in through the windows. They were not officers. These soldiers had the eager and malicious grins of children who enjoy poking wounded animals with a stick and the giddy excitement that leached from their every movement permeated the air of the room with a sickening aura of expectation.

I knew this would not end well, and the rising and falling of Xinyi's shoulders told me that fear had begun to take control of her. For my own part, I tried to control my emotions, though I knew that would be used and beaten and scorned for an indiscernible amount of time. Nothing and no one would come to our aid no matter how long we waited, and the feeling of desperation, coupled with the moans of Japanese soldiers and the frightful screams of Chinese women and children that reached our ears, made me feel queasy as well. I had a lump in my throat and I sat in perfect stillness, hoping they would leave us alone. But, of course, this would not be the case.

The first soldier lunged for Xinyi and she kicked him in the groin with an animal shout. The pain doubled the man over, sending his hat falling to the ground, and he crawled away with his pathetic Japanese wails reaching the ceiling and circling all around us. Again, more soldiers grabbed at Xinyi and, despite her efforts to fight them off, she was eventually swallowed up in the wave of uniforms that rose to enshroud her. I tried to fight as well but the soldiers would not be stopped. It was as if the long war in a terrible condition had unlocked something inhuman in their characters, something beyond anything I had seen.

I gave up the fight before Xinyi did. I tried to block out the sounds of their grunting and moaning and the undulating whines that they sent up to the heavens every time one of the Japanese devils finished their business. To me it was becoming routine, but the pounding in my head would not abate and, as my face was pushed into the hardwood, the abrasions from the previous day began to ooze blood out of my crotch that smelt of nickel. It will be over soon.

That's what I told myself and, when Xinyi managed to turn her head toward me, I tried to look away, but the terror in her eyes held me rapt. It will be over soon. And it was. At least, I think it was. I have no recollection of how long it took them to sate their evil desires nor how many Japanese raped us.

But in the end, they grew bored and walked away, leaving us to sob silently in each other's clutches as I stroked her hair. As I tried to comfort Xinyi, a face that I had dreamed of so many times in the recent weeks and months appeared before me and, when I looked up, I saw someone familiar. I saw Dong E. But when our gazes met, I recognized the same sense of bewilderment that I knew must have been painted over my own face—the way her lips hung open just so, the way her head was tilted slightly to one side, and her eyes wide open—and the realization that Dong E was still alive and in the same camp as myself sank in.

"Huh—, Dong E... I never—" The syllables stammered their way out as if someone else had taken control of my voice and forgot how to speak. For her part, Dong E did not manage to articulate anything more impressive.

"Kuaishou," she began, but said nothing else after that, as if the disbelief of seeing me had taken away her eloquence.

"Dong E, we have so much... we need to..."

She shot furtive glances over both shoulders and then took the robes she had been carrying and draped them over our naked, sweaty bodies. She moved quickly, with a deft agility that made me think she had been here for a long time and that she was being trained for something. She acted like a hotel magnate in Beijing would. Dignified. Her makeup and face paint made her rounded, soft features seem sharp, like those of a golden eagle, and the look in her eyes had the same predatory nature. I did not know what had befallen her but I knew instantly that it wouldn't be good.

"We do not know each other," she said. "If they think we know each other, they will separate us again." It felt wonderful for us to see her. I had many questions that I could not ask at the moment. If life could have frozen forever in that moment, I think that perhaps the entire road of pain and suffering may have been worthwhile.

"And who is she?" Dong E asked.

"She is my cell mate. My friend."

"Xinyi Sung," she said, saying her own name as if for the first time. "I have been here for fifty two days."

"I've been instructed to attend to you two," Dong E said, shame in her voice. "The commandant has ordered me to be the groomer of his slaves, the manager of this infernal pleasure camp."

Dong E, whose voice was saturated with the venom of betrayal and hatred, spat silently on the floor when she spoke the words. Then, she kept on speaking: "These are your robes, your clothes. I will show you to your new quarters, which are slightly better than the rocks they keep the new girls in. I am so sorry that we are all here, but at least we are here together."

Dong E brought Xinyi to her new quarters—scarcely more than a broom closet with a frayed sleeping pad and no windows—and left her to mourn the loss of her dignity in solace. When she began to lead me through the convoluted maze of the pleasure house, I tried my hardest to take note of every turn, every window, every point of entry or escape, but the pounding in my head was getting worse with every passing step; I could not keep my bearing in the endlessly twisting corridors that all looked exactly the same. Dong E whispered in a low voice as we walked, constantly shifting her gaze back and forth and looking over her shoulders to make sure that no Japanese were watching or following.

"The Eighth Route Army was losing, I hear," she said, the news sounding as if she were reporting on the weather. "There has been no news, but rumors are circulating that some of the fighters have made it to Jingui and are taking shelter here among sympathizers—." We turned a corner and she dropped the conversation as two Japanese soldiers walked toward us, stared at us like pieces of meat, and kept walking to whatever post they were supposed to be manning. When they had disappeared around the corner, we began our furtive conversation again.

She told me all about the war or, at least, as much as she knew. The Eighth Route Army had been on the run for some time, and the superior fire power of the Japanese soldiers was constantly beating back any attempts to sabotage their advance. Informants littered the villages and no Chinese could ever be sure that the words they whispered to a neighbor in secret would not, in turn, be whispered to the Japanese the following morning. Executions. Villages burned.

Rapes and kidnappings and sex slavery. All of what we expect from the Japanese.

When she showed me to my new room, she held out a blanket with an ornate, intricate pattern dancing across it, and the splendor of its vivid dye caught my attention and brought a smile to my face even in these dire circumstances. "This blanket used to belong to Hou Datu," she said. "It is the only piece of evidence I have that the Eighth Route Army has actually made it into Jingui, but it could have been stolen or taken off his dead body."

The mention of Hou Datu's name brought a smile to my face just as the blanket brought warmth to my heart. He was a legendary fighter with the Eighth Route Army, the pride of our province when the rumors began to circulate that he was joining the fray. An expert demolitions man, he was responsible for countless bridge bombings and, almost single handedly, prevented the Japanese from totally running over the Communist forces in the northeast.

Despite this, his reputation for humility and modesty traveled even further than his predilections for war and plastic explosives. When people would crowd around him and offer praise and recognition and extra pork for his valorous service and dedication to China's greatness, he would demur and look down at the ground with a scarred and mutilated hand help up to stop the accolades. "I am only a man. We are all China," he would say with the wisdom of a sage.

That night I tried to sleep through the sounds of rape and the shrieks of pain that diffused themselves through the thin walls like the chill of the night winds cutting through the village from the peak of the mountain. Pulling the blanket tight around my frame, I thought about Dong E and the manner in which she addressed me, the rigid formality of her posture and the cold, seemingly uncaring tone that she employed when speaking about the destruction of the Eighth Route Army.

Was it an artifice? A construct so the Japanese dogs would not suspect her or her allegiances? Or did her experiences break her entirely and tear down the pillars that had kept her indomitable will propped up? Did she have a plan or had she given up? These questions brought up new questions, and the new questions brought up still new considerations that plagued my mind and kept me tossing on the mat they had thrown into my quarters. At least I had a window and the blanket and Dong E and Xinyi Sung.

I stared out the window at the clouds that pushed their way up from the valley and enshrouded the mountain top in a haze of mist and fog. The moon peeked through, barely a pale spot in the gathering clouds, but it was enough to push through and cast a sickly light on the surrounding hovels and huts and buildings with pillars of smoke rising from their chimneys. From these heights, one might be convinced that the scene before me was one of idyllic pleasure in the mountains, a life to be jealous of, covetous of. Only when one got closer to the action did it become clear that this mountain had become a tortured place, where enmity and hatred ruled over the passions of the inhabitants.

I looked out the window for a long time, hugging the blanket that from Hou Datu that Dong E had given me. I stared down at the ground, muddy and smeared and damp in the night. Probably two or three lis off the ground. Without any warning, the thought exploded into my mind: How bad would it hurt? Certainly I wouldn't be able to run and escape if I dropped myself out of the window and made a sprint for the tree line. I'd be gunned down in a second.

A cold wind kicked up, chilling me and causing me to hug the blanket even closer, to squeeze it as if it were my daughter. But if I tied this piece of cloth to something? If I could drop down from three or four meters instead of five or six? Then, perhaps, I would be free. Truly free. I could return with the Eighth Route Army to liberate this cave, and the final thing I would do would be to put a Chinese bullet between the commandant's eyes. The thought warmed my heart at the same time it startled me. I had never been such a violent person, though the image of killing the commandant would not leave my mind and, instead, took over everything until I lapsed into a tortured sleep, dreams of Hou Datu, Dong E and Wuxiao barraging me with emotional, falsified memories.

Chapter 12

FALL HAD DESERTED THE VALLEYS below us and left nothing but blankets of snow and spoiled crops in its wake. The Japanese, in their insolence and depravity, spent the transitional season chopping down trees, splitting great piles of splintered wood to burn in their camps, and stealing food from the locals who had no food even for their own families. When the first flurries gave way to furious blizzards, with winds kicking ice crystals up into the air and toppling dead trees, they redoubled their efforts. Before long, great caravans of wagons, carts, dollies and anything else with wheels proceeded up the winding and precarious pass that led to our camp. Their storage trunks were piled with yams, soybeans, carrots, and heavy bags of wheat that caused the hungry peasants to groan with exertion every time one was lifted from the horse drawn carts of a villager and throw haphazardly into the canvas covered automobiles that rumbled and coughed black smoke from their tail pipes.

From my barred window, I watched, taking note of the monotonous and unchanging faces of the villagers. Every one of them, bent into a grimace of discomfort, exertion and hatred. Through the snow muffled the sound, the barking orders of Japanese soldiers reached my ears, as did the barking of dogs, the mewling of cattle, and the whinny of goats brought into the camp to be butchered for the soldiers.

When the first real snowstorm hit the mountaintop, it struck hard, blowing in quick and blanketing the entire mountain and valleys below with an impassable covering of snow that made the pass a death trap, causing more than one donkey or ox to slip off the trail, sliding with a groan of terror before going over the precipices and into the chasm below, dragging with them carrots, potatoes, and the grain that the Japanese demanded. To make matters worse, the previous spring had been dry and many fields cracked and blistered in heat that swept over the region, so when harvest season fell upon the villagers, many had to wring stale dirt between their fingers and look to the sky with unspoken questions burning in their eyes. Why? How? How to go on, with the Japanese insisting on their extortioner's bounty and no food even in the larder?

One by one, the villagers ceased coming to the camp, and the soldiers—who throughout the fall had been boisterous and intent on rousting every Chinese girl they could find from her hiding place and performing all manner of unspeakable atrocities upon her—grew weary, flustered, agitated. Scared. I saw it in their faces when they would order me into bed. I heard it in their discontented groans as they rocked themselves to an unsatisfying orgasm.

And I was disgusted. Every time a Japanese soldier struck me or one of my camp comrades out of frustration because they were too far from home, too long at war, too hungry to even have the energy to rape properly, my soul felt a brief moment of respite, and my heart knew contentment at last. They were not cut out for this life—the life of a hardscrabble peasant in the hinterlands of China, where nothing came easy and everything demanded the utmost exaction.

As the winter grew deeper and deeper and the sun remained behind dense, gunmetal clouds for days at a time, freezing temperatures began claiming toes, noses, fingers and feet, and the soldiers milling around the camp became vicious and factional. Fights broke out in the bread lines and more than one soldier found himself blindfolded against the pine walls of the fortress, waiting for the deafening gunshots that would splatter his innards on the wall behind him. The porters from the village below the mountaintop were fewer and fewer and their provisions worse with every passing visit.

One day, as I watched the soldiers carting in the peasants' crop—only a few strong men, with burly shoulders that made them look as if they had been farming for their entire lives—I noticed a man who stood aside from the rest. His musculature, even from this distance, was easily evident beneath his tattered tunic and, unlike the rest of the villagers, he did not avert his eyes from the gaze of the Japanese commissary officer who arrogantly checked off the list every piece of produce that was brought up to the fortress. The others hid their eyes, looked at the frozen ground, and shifted their weight from side to side as the officers dug through their larders, but this man stared impassively at the commissary man and refused to be intimidated when they threatened him or otherwise hassled him or his young child.

"That is Zheng Menghai," Dong E said to me in a low whisper as she dampened a cloth with warm water, to ease the bruises left behind by the last soldier who visited me in the night. "He is in the party," she added in a low, conspiratorial whisper.

"He had much food," I said, my mouth watering as the fires began to burn with enthusiasm below. In the fortress courtyard, the soldiers struggled against the beating, kicking, fighting spirit of a horse that had bones sticking out of his frame in stark relief. Zheng Menghai said nothing nor did he offer to help. The horse—who would undoubtedly be roasting over the fragrant fire before the sun went down—had likely belonged to him, though I never would have guessed that by the stolid demeanor he levelled at his foes. It aroused a sort of inspiration in me. For a man to part ways with his horse in such a horrid fashion made me wonder what else had happened to him, what other tragedies he had borne with a silent conviction and an unchanging face.

"He has been smuggling food for us women," my friend said, her voice even lower than when she had confided his party allegiances. I turned toward Dong E, her outstretched arm holding a dark brown, overripe chunk of pumpkin, its sinuous fibers leaking a viscous fluid that reminded me of stomach bile. It made me want to wretch, but it also made me want to bite off Dong E's hand with it. I had not eaten fresh produce in many nights, and I did not know when the next chance would come around.

She broke the morsel in two and we both nibbled in silence, keeping an eye cast toward the door, hoping that no one would interrupt our meal. After we finished eating, she told me that she had to see Xinyi, who had been beaten by the guards for biting too hard and would need the aid of a trained medicine master before she ever opened her right eye again.

"Is she okay?" I asked.

"She is getting by. Tough as the hide of an ox, that one."

And she left me with my thoughts, my fears, my forebodings that as the winter progressed, the severity of our famine would only get worse. I wondered how long we would be able to count on men like Zheng Menghai and what the Japanese dogs would do to him if he were ever caught.

The room they kept me in became my new prison. Barren and void of anything reminiscent of home, the hard floor was cold to touch with my feet and the window constantly let in gusts of cold air that chilled my spine as I tried to sleep. Captivity is even worse than the terrors of war, I realized. Or, maybe, captivity was the quintessential terror that war had to offer. When you thought your moment of respite had finally arrived, you realize that it is nothing more than crippling boredom. I passed my days by watching the clouds, thinking about Nainai—assuming she was dead—and wondering if Wuxiao had ever even bothered to look for me when I failed to show up with his grandmother.

Food became scarce and the soldiers angrier, more desperate to abuse any one of us and more depraved in their sexual tastes. I performed untold acts of perversion for them that I will not recount ever again and have struggled for long years to bury in the many textured memories that the war affords me. But one night, when I lay in a deep chill, struggling to sleep, a great commotion shook me from my thoughts and opened my eyes wide with the tenor of clamor and agitation. I heard women screaming and the bellowing of a soldier that sounded as if he had been shot through the gut with a machine gun round. His screams undulated and echoed through the passages of the fortress and, when I poked my head out of the door, I saw that the other women on the second floor of the pleasure house had done the same, attracted by the great catastrophe that had apparently befallen one of the soldiers in the night.

That is when I saw the man. He stumbled out of Xinyi's room, his hand cupped over his left eye and when, I looked more closely at the staggering, enraged, terrified man, I noticed the thin rivulet of dark red blood that trickled between his fingers. When he looked up—not at me, but in my direction—and moved his hands, I saw a thin sliver of wood, a chopstick perhaps, jutting from the cavity where his eye had been. His good eye was wide with fear, surprise, and pain. They all blended together into a look that only wounded animals can sincerely muster.

Out of the room behind him, Xinyi was swinging her balled fists at the man's back, bellowing in rage and indignation. She did not even make any words as she shouted and hammered at the disoriented soldier's back, but I knew exactly what she had meant to say. "Go home. Leave us be and never return. Please." Behind her, Dong E tried to hold back my friend, but nothing would stop the woman from beating the wounded soldier and slinging invective at him. "Please, Xinyi," Dong E began, though her words were cut off by the tormented screaming of the other two. "Please, this isn't going to end well..."

From out of nowhere—and everywhere—the Japanese fell on the two of them, beat them with rifles and pistol butts, kicked them, and spat on them. Dong E covered her face and took the blows, but Xinyi was implacable. She continued to wail on the man until the soldiers finally subdued her, and the commandant emerged, firing his pistol into the air and leaving us in a wake of silence and gun smoke that drifted down the hall and danced about the lamps that hung outside of every door.

A soldier came out to shout out commands. Although I had no idea what he was saying, muted rage was seeping from every syllable. The soldier, who had ceased screaming and only moaned softly against the palms of his bloodstained hands, was led away. He turned to Dong E and Xinyi. Without breaking his gaze, he said to the remaining soldiers, something such as, "Take them, too. Back to the caves." He walked away then and that was it. As the soldiers led the two women away, I stared into both of their gazes and they stared back. Dong E's face? The picture of fear and alarm—eyes wide and cheeks pale, lips trembling as she walked past my door without looking back. At that moment, I knew that I would never see her again. The commandant shouted for everyone to retire to their quarters and we all did as we were told.

I did not sleep for even a moment that night but, rather, laid awake thinking about the retribution that would be rained down on all of us in the upcoming days, weeks, months.

After Xinyi Sung had blinded a Japanese soldier in one eye, the soldiers were both wary and brutal towards us. They didn't know what we had planned, what we wanted to do to them as they raped us and bruised us and beat us. Throughout the camp, as the winter grew colder, so too did the atmosphere inside the pleasure house. No more did the soldiers laugh as they raped us. Rather, their brutal, animalistic sex became something of revenge.

After a few days, we were all summoned into the courtyard, led by soldiers with carbines and pistols levelled at our heads, barking in their broken Mandarin that anyone who tried anything at all would be summarily executed. We pretended we did not know what was going on, but I think that every one of the women in that camp knew what we were being summoned for. I know I did. I knew for certain that such an offense as Xinyi had committed would not be forgotten easily and that reparations were in order.

We huddled together trying to bunch up the fabric around ourselves and tucked our hands into our armpits for warmth. I tried not to shiver, tried to show the Japanese how a real soldier handles the bitter cold, but the icy gusts were too much for me to handle in such skimpy, ill-fitting clothes and, before long, I joined the rest of the girls, shivering pathetically. Snow was falling, though it had not grown into a squall yet. I knew it would but, for now, a light flurry fell on the ground, adding to the drifts where the peasants had been made to shovel walkways.

We stood in the cold for a long time or so it felt. And by the time I heard one of the women say, "Look over there! It's Xinyi Sung!" I knew that we were about to witness an execution. I had seen many terrors in my time on the run and in the pleasure camp, but I had never seen a friend die. I turned my head toward the gate of the compound and I saw her—Xinyi Sung, who had been so strong, so fierce when I first was brought to this camp, who had instilled a sense of bravery and comradery in me, was now being led by the muzzle of a rifle with her hands and feet shackled. She looked like a pale impression of her former self; her hair stood up and bunched together where it had knotted, and the bruises that she already suffered on her face seemed to have swollen and had taken over her entire body. She was black and blue and purple and yellow with the color of beaten flesh, and her head bobbed up and down as she limped along barefoot in the snow. But her head was not down. She stared straight ahead, with empty eyes that seemed to take in everything and nothing at the same time. Eyes of a spirit, wandering in the world of man.

They marched her up to the wall and pushed her forcefully against the timbers, which resonated with the thud of her body slamming against them. She almost fell but, at the last moment, she succeeded in maintaining her footing and righted her posture against the wall. I do not know for sure but, to this day, I feel she was looking straight at me, her gaze boring through my own and penetrating the deepest emotions that I had long ago learned to banish.

The commandant strode before us, eyeing each one of us the way he did when he was appraising which one of us he wanted in his bed that night. But he had none of the sickening sense of pleasure that polluted his mien on those nights. His jaw was set, his eyes piercing, his voice booming when he screamed over the rising wind.

"Today, you will all learn what happens to communists, communist sympathizers, and whores who cannot learn their place. Today, we will show you why Japan is the greatest empire the world has seen and why your pathetic homeland is just another one on our list of conquests."

He took a breath and his exhalation was like the billowing smoke from a malevolent dragon as it flew away on the breeze.

"A new order starts today. When you are crying at night, when you are wishing it would all be over, when you contemplate killing yourself solely for the purpose of escaping my wrath, you have her to thank." His finger stuck out in Xinyi's direction, though he would not grace her with a stare. He kept his gaze trained on us for a minute, two minutes... who knew? It felt like an eternity, as if he had become a statue or as if the wind and the snow had frozen him in place.

"Soldiers!" he shouted, and the words were carried off by the gathering storm before they had the chance to echo. The soldiers lined up with their back to us and loaded their rifles. Turning to Xinyi Sung for the first time, he asked her with a sneer in his eyes and spittle on his lips if she had any last words. Xinyi Sung looked up toward the clouds, which were a uniform color, and which passed by the drama playing out below them without a care. "The National Revolutionary Army will turn all of your mothers and sisters and daughters into..."

But the words were cut off by the resounding crack of nine rifle shots that echoed through the evening sky. I tried not to look, but in the end, I could not avert my gaze as the rigid posture of Xinyi Sung gave way to the chaotic, infinitesimally short dance of death that all gunshot victims acted out. I heard simultaneously the reports of the gunshots and the sickening thumping sound of the bullets hitting her torso in nine different places, the louder thud of her body being thrown against the wall, the soft, almost sensual sound of the snow being pushed around as her frame slumped over in a pile, blood staining the ground around her and the wall behind her. The last image I have of her is of her eyes and her smile, for it is true that, despite the horror of the lives we Chinese lived, Xinyi Sung died with a song on her lips and a smile in her heart. Her head was pointed up at the clouds. Just like them, she no longer cared.

Chapter 13

WINTER HAD NEVER PASSED so slowly and, without my friends Dong E or Xinyi Sung to alleviate the alternating periods of boredom and terror, I had nothing to do but watch the snow pile up in great drifts and listen to the interminable howling of the wind over the chasms that surrounded us in between the soldiers' visits. At night, as the gusts and gales passed by my eaves, I listened for the voices from my past and took comfort in knowing that at least the winds were an unchanging, inalterable force that would not leave me alone. I bided my time. I slept with the soldiers who knocked on my door at night, though they came with deteriorating frequency, as if my despondency ruined their fun.

Rumors passed through the pleasure camp that Dong E had been raped to death, that she had been decapitated, that she had been fed to the wolves that were encroaching with greater ease on our campgrounds, but I did not believe them. When I watched Xinyi Sung breathe her last, I felt her death like an evacuation of spirit, as if a piece of my own life had been killed in a hail of bullets as well, and I did not feel any such emptiness when I thought about Dong E. She was probably in the caves below the fortress or else had been brought to a new pleasure camp. She could have been rescued.

Anything could have happened, but I knew she was alive, and the thought of her torment kept me awake at night, wringing the blanket, and planning for my escape. Though I knew it had to happen soon, I knew that, if I didn't get off this rock, I would end up snapping like Xinyi Sung and, if that happened, I would surely take at least one Japanese with me. Poor Xinyi. She aimed for the eyeball when she had a clear opening for the man's neck. I wouldn't be so careless. I f I was going to throw my life away, it was going to be for something more than merely blinding my enemy in one eye.

Just as surely as I knew that I needed to escape and soon, I also knew that I could not possibly make it out of the fortress and down to the village below during a winter like this. Every day, the snow piled up and my hopes were soon buried in it, frozen under a mound of ice and waiting for the rejuvenating spring thaw. To pass the time in some useful endeavor, I began to count the Japanese soldiers on the base and, though their ranks were constantly changing as new units were brought in to rest, and the old ones shipped out to do more killing, pillaging and raping, I figured that the base held about one hundred soldiers at any given time. Those were tough odds, I knew. But I also knew that I would rather get shot in the back running down the hill, away from this frozen hell. From my window, I could see the main gates, and I began keeping track of the guards and their movements and the times at which they changed shifts. Once in the morning, shortly after the gruel that passed for a morning meal, and once after dinner, as the sun was impaling itself and the fangs of the western mountain ranges and painting the sky with its varicolored blood of oranges, purple, reds and yellows.

That would have to be the time, I surmised, though the brutality of the temperatures at night would kill me about as fast as a Japanese bullet. I had heard stories of people who froze to death when they got lost in the mountains in my own province, and everyone talked about how their bodies were found with a serene smile painted over their faces, as if they had some stunning realizations as they drew their final breath. It made me think about Xinyi Sung, which always made my eyes well up with salty tears that would sting my bruises if I let them spill over.

It was during these brutal winter months, around the time when one unit of soldiers went back to the front and another cycled into the pleasure camp, that I met him—a Japanese soldier who had a narrow face, kind eyes, and a childish expression on his face at all times, as if he were not a soldier at war employed in the act of killing strangers. I noticed him immediately because his disposition differed so greatly from any of the other soldiers who had intruded on my cave during the night. He smiled. He had no scars, and was not as rough as the others. Mostly, he stuck out because he spoke Mandarin and always carried a tiny book around with him.

He was more gentle than the rest, when he began to slide closer to me. I must admit that I felt a flush in my cheeks when his penetrating gaze met my own. He was courting me. I wanted to slap him in the face and scream at him that he only needed to rip my clothes off and have his way like all the others, but the great sorrow that I read in his eyes melted my hardened exterior defenses—which I had worked so hard to build up in the aftermath of Xinyi Sung's execution. When his hand fell gently on my thigh, much like the snow that danced its way to the ground or dead leaves in the autumn harvest season, I let it rest there and covered it with my own. We stared at each other, communicating in silence as our lips drew closer together. Soon, we were locked in each other's embrace, rolling around the kang and letting our hands wander wherever they wanted to go. I felt him caressing the small of my back, the inside of my thighs, the curvature of my breasts, and my own hands gliding over his chest, his abdomen, his face where the stubble grew around his jawline and tickled my soft palms. That night, for the first time in my life, I made love with another man, and when I woke up in the morning, he was already gone, leaving me to wonder if my soul had not been corrupted by a strange Japanese demon.

But I continued to see him around the base and, in the evenings, I would stare at his silhouette when he hunched over by the gate reading his book. I dreamed of him and imagined that he dreamed of me. He continued to come to my room and, when we laid together, our tryst soon took on a forbidden aspect, as if he would be executed if the commandant found him loving a Chinese woman instead of raping her. Others would come into my quarters during the night and their rapid, short-lived thrusting destroyed my peace, the serenity that I felt when he was inside me. I wondered how it made him feel, to have fallen in love with a whore, because I felt for sure that this is what happened. It was written in the somber hue of his eyes and the delicate touch of his fingertips on my womanhood.

He brought me food at night—much better food than any that can be spared on a Chinese whore, and this I sincerely did think would lead to his death if he had been caught. After I had eaten half a carrot that he had smuggled from the mess in his boot, we lay in silence, and I asked him: "Why are you doing this?"

"Because you are, to me, a goddess. You don't deserve this. None of you."

"No," I said. "Why are you *this*? Carrying a gun, fighting a war, obeying your commands? Do you believe in it?"

He sighed and his gaze wandered out of the window toward the mountains beyond the confining walls of the camp. "Sometimes, we are given a choice. Other times, we aren't. It is that simple. I have a wife and children. If I did not go to war, they would be shamed, and we would be outcasts."

I must admit that, despite the adamant hatred I fostered for the Japanese, this man had pierced my heart, and his revelation squashed the amorous feelings that had begun to erode my stolid serenity. I said nothing in response but held him tightly because I knew that, very shortly, the soldiers would be rotated out of the camp and he would be gone from my life like the others, like Xinyi Sung, Xiao Si, and Wuxiao. We made love for the last time that night. Our act was followed by an awkward silence, laden with sorrow, and he left shortly after, looking back at me with the same solemn eyes that had captivated me from the beginning.

Dong E surprised me as the winter was nearing its end by showing up in the pleasure camp again. Her face looked as if it had just finished healing from a severe beating and her attitude reminded me of that of a wild animal terrified to have woken up in captivity. She was skittish and barely spoke a word and, when I greeted her with a smile on my face and exuberance hanging from every word, she only looked at me with a broken gaze that shook me to my core.

I pulled her into my quarters and grabbed her by the shoulders, squaring her up and inspecting her from head to toe. "Dong E," I said, feeling like a child again, "It is so great to see you alive again. I thought for sure..." I didn't finish the statement. It had been three months since Xinyi

Sung had stabbed a man through the eye with a chopstick, three months since Dong E was sent away and tortured.

Finally, after a moment of silence, she addressed me.

"Kuaishou, though I am standing before you, you must know that I died on that day when Xinyi Sung was marched before the wall. Something inside me was killed by those bullets, just as surely as our friend was, and I fear I will never be the same again." I held her close and rubbed her back with my hands, stared into her eyes with only centimeters of space between our faces.

"It is over, Dong E. It is over. You made it." I repeated this many times, though I doubt Dong E believed it. For that matter, I doubted whether I believed it myself.

We sat in silence, for I could think of nothing to say that would assuage the deep pain that had consumed Dong E. She broke the silence first.

"Hey," she said, dropping her voice so that no one would hear her whispering in my ear, "How are your plans for escape going?"

I looked at her with grave severity and then shot a glance over to the door. I walked over toward the hallway and peaked out. No soldiers. No girls. I sat beside Dong E again and reached down to the floor, working my fingernails into one of the grooves between the boards. When I pried it loose, I pulled out Hou Datu's blanket, torn into thick strips and now refashioned as a long, strong rope.

"This will reach the ground. Though I do not know if

we can survive the cold and I do not know how we will get through the gates."

"We must try. They will kill all of us before they move on. I know this now. The Japanese are a depraved people. They will do it for fun. There is another door, on the other side of the camp. The commandant's adjutants go through there on secret assignments and only one guard mans it at night. Tonight, I will sneak into your room after the dogs have finished with their bones."

I nodded in silence to her and she left my side. A great wave of anxiety swept over me as I waited for the sun to go down. One by one the soldiers came to my door and had their way with me and, every time, finished with their forceful stabbing.

The last soldier spilt his seed with a disgusting grimace on his face and left without a word. Better that way. I had things to do. The moment his footsteps faded down the hall, I fervently pried the loose floorboard from my secret hiding spot and removed the blanket, which was now a rope, my ticket to freedom, and other rags and cloths that I had succeeded in pilfering during my stay at the camp. I put them onto my body, trying to insulate myself as much as I could, and wrapped my feet with the rest of the bandages and cloths I had. A cold wind cut in through the window, bringing a dusting of snow with it that melted on the floor. I saw it as a bad omen but nothing would stop me tonight. By the time Dong E had slipped silently into my room, I had already tied the blanket rope to the support beam that was exposed by the loose floorboard. I had no idea if it would hold or if the rope would snap and leave one of us, or both of us, paralyzed in the snow beneath the window.

"We are ready," Dong E said, and there was not even a hint of a question in her voice. I nodded to her and embraced her with a hug that seemed to squeeze the air out of her lungs. She hugged me back and, when we broke our embrace, we stared into each other's eyes for a few seconds before I broke the silence.

"You first?" She nodded and pulled on the rope with great force. The beam it was attached to let out a sickening groan that I feared would wake up the entire camp but our decision had already been made. It was time to leave this life behind forever. I spared one thought for Xinyi before Dong E swung her leg over the window sill and disappeared from sight. She deftly lowered herself to the snow without a sound and waited for me to follow but, suddenly, from up high on the ledge the height seemed impossible, and my vision began to swim as I thought about following Dong E's lead.

"Come on," she whispered in a harsh voice. She said something else but the rising wind obscured it. Now or never. I threw my right leg over the sill, gave the rope one last tug, and began to lower myself to the ground below. Already my fingers went numb and, as I inched my way down, the groaning strain of my weight on the rope rattled around in my ears and my face flushed with fear and exhilaration. I had almost made it. The ground was so close.

Suddenly, as I was approaching the ground, the blanket gave way and, with a shriek of surprise and fear, I plummeted to the ground and hit the snow bank with a great plume that rose up and danced around us in the wind.

"Shhh!" Dong E whispered. "Quiet, or they'll hear us."

I recovered from the fall, though my heart was racing, and I felt it beating against my ribcage like that of a rabbit chased by dogs. After I stood up from the snowbank—soaking wet and shivering—we crept in the shadows along the foundation of the fort, me following Dong E's lead. At the southwest corner of the compound, we came to the open expanse of a snowy courtyard.

"What do we do?" I asked.

"We run."

She counted to three and, on the final number, the two of us, hand in hand, took off toward the wall with high, chopping strides as we struggled against the depth of the snow. I had never felt so naked in my life. I didn't want to spare even a second to look behind me or to scan the walls for watchers. I only wanted to keep my eyes trained on our destination—the tiny door on the other side of the courtyard. We had almost made the run when I heard the voice shouting behind us and my heart sank.

"Stop! Hold it right there!" came the broken Mandarin from a Japanese soldier.

"Faster!" Dong E shouted, and we lurched through the deep snow, breaking into a zig zag pattern as the first rifle cracks broke the stillness of the night. One shot fired after another and, before long, a barrage of bullets rained down around us, whistling past our ears and kicking up tufts of snow in the night. But we made it. We finally made it.

With the full force of our momentum, Dong E and I slammed into the door and it gave way as if it were made of paper. We spilled into the snow on the other side of the wall and, for the first time in months, I felt free air filling my lungs. But we were not free yet.

"Freeze! Right now!" screamed the soldier who was watching the door. He leveled a rifle at us and his whole body trembled, though from fear or the gripping cold, I could not discern. His voice sounded familiar, but I had no time to think about anything. The soldiers inside were being rounded up and, before long, they would fall upon us and we would be marched against the wall like Xinyi Sung. Without a moment's thought to spare, we both charged at his shoulder and fell upon him, gnashing at him, scratching and punching him. He got one shot off, but it went wild, flying into the night sky.

He cried for us to stop, but we would not listen. Finally, I reached for a rock on the ground where we rolled in the snow, fighting for our lives, and I raised it high above my head. That is when the man turned his face toward me. I had no time to think and, with my eyes closed tightly against the horror, I brought the rock down. I felt bones cracking underneath the rock's weight and the sound it made sickened my stomach. I brought the rock down again and again, until Dong E pulled me from his body and dragged me into the tree line, into my new life. I spared one last look over my shoulder as the rifle shots from the guards whizzed by us, slamming into tree trunks and peppering us with splinters. We made it. The darkness of the forest swallowed us up and, before long, the pleasure camp disappeared behind us.

Though we had escaped from the pursuing soldiers—who hollered at us and sent bullets whizzing by our ears as we stumbled, terrified, through the darkened forest—that night our travails were not yet over. The moon, which had been shining clear and bright and full when we had sprinted through the courtyard, had retreated behind a thick cover of swollen clouds, promising snow. We could see nothing and constantly scraped our flesh against tree branches and briars that snagged our ill-fitting obis and threatened to unravel them. Slightly ahead of me, I heard the grunting of Dong E and, though she sounded as if she were only just in front of me, I could not make out even her faintest silhouette or shadow and felt utterly and completely alone.

As the branches in front of me continued to snap and creak and bend, I knew that Dong E was getting ahead of me and I had to fight against the urge to call out to her. The voices of the Japanese were still audible and, though they sounded as if they had given up the chase, it would not alert them as to our direction. We cut back and forth through the forest, the grade of the forest floor growing increasingly steep, until I became positive that Dong E did not know where she was going at all but had acted on pure instinct. When the voices of the soldiers and reports of the wild rifle shots had faded into the dark chasm of the night, I chanced to call her name. I stopped running, rested my legs by leaning against the bark of a bushy fir tree, and called out as quietly as I could through ragged, uneven breaths.

"Dong E!" I called, in a strange and foreign voice that somehow mimicked both a whisper and a desperate shout at the same time. "Where are you?" Stillness, then, and no sound save the rhythmic rising and falling of my breasts as my lungs struggled to recoup. I doubled over, feeling the electric, animalistic sensation of fear welling up from deep within my stomach. When I was running through the forest, blindly, terrified, dodging bullets, I had been able to keep out the freezing sensation of the snow biting into the soles of my feet, but now, with my heart rate slowing, I felt once more the commingled pain and numbness that accompanied being practically bare-foot in the snow.

"Dong E," I tried again, a little louder, my voice shaking. I hated the sound of it reverberating through the woods and reaching my ears again as an echo. I could sense the fear in that sound and I knew it would kill me in the end. So would standing still, I decided. I started out again, arms extended out before me, feeling the lash and tickle of evergreen boughs slapping against my face, my hands, my torso. I moved slowly, taking care to place my feet exactly where they needed to go, every step. More than once, a lucky grab at an unseen branch in the dark prevented me from tumbling down the increasingly steep slope. I felt like I was on the side of a mountain, and the absence of the strong gales that continuously blew up higher on the mountain was the only thing that kept me from falling down and rolling into... who knew?

I continued to call out for Dong E. I stumbled, tripped, screamed. Gravity seemed to have forgotten about me, and the lurch in my stomach produced a wave of nausea as my feet slid out from under me and I felt my sense of direction turn on its head. I had sure footing, for a second, and then, just like that, I was toppling over, somersaulting down the mountain and sliding through the snow and ice, desperately reaching out to grab anything at all—a tree root, a stump a rock, a crevice—anything that was flying past me that would afford something to grasp.

But I found nothing and continued to crash down the slope for what felt like minutes, but for what surely was no more than a dozen or so feet of bouncing off the forest floor and struggling to keep in the pain and fear that the sensation of falling had produced. When I came to a stop on a flat portion of the forest floor—a road of some sort, old and forgotten, possibly for logging—I found that I had come to a rest right where Dong E was crouched in the shadows.

She grabbed me and covered my mouth, looking around with furtive glances as if we were being stalked by a beast of the field. In a sense, I suppose we were. Who knew if the Japanese had truly given up or if they had just gotten quiet? My careening fall down the remainder of the slope that led away from the pleasure camp surely would have attracted the attention of anything—anyone—in the forest. We sat perfectly still, so long that a thin layer of snow began to form on the crown of Dong E's raven black hair. We both shivered and bit the sides of our mouths to fight off the cold and prevent our teeth from chattering too loudly.

Looking around, my initial impression was correct. We had found a road. It was wide enough to fit no more than one cart and a couple of donkeys. "Which way?" I asked. "I didn't think we'd make it this far..." Dong E confessed and we lapsed back into silence. With the cold seeping into every centimeter of my body and breaking my voice into a strangled series of syllables, I picked the direction. South. I had had enough of the mountains for a lifetime and, if I was ever to find Wuxiao again, it was the only direction to travel.

We hadn't made it more than a quarter li before we received a great shock, and both of us nearly stumbled off the advancing deterioration of the road and back into the forest. It started as a strange noise from the woods— big enough to be a bear, but too steady and too fast. It was a constant rhythm. Not a bear, no. Humans.

Even in the dark, I felt Dong E staring at me, hoping I would appear just as terrified as she did. The sound came closer and, for an absurd moment of panic, we were frozen. The cold had been banished by the sudden kick of nerves, but we were frozen, nonetheless. Footsteps not crashing through the woods, but proceeding cautiously, carefully. They were meters away and getting closer. Finally, I pulled on Dong E's elbow and we fit into the cavity of a fir tree's canopy, so deep that even the blizzards of this winter had not reached its bottom. We sat there and waited. I was sure we would be stuck and hated myself for even thinking about jumping into the pit, but as the footsteps drew even closer, and their voices became distinguishable, I felt my heart begin to hammer.

In a quiet, slow voice, perfectly accented and bastardized Mandarin.

"Bullets?" No response. Just the sound of ammunition cartridges exchanging hands in the darkness. The footsteps had the rhythm of a lullaby and their voices were as calm as a lake in midsummer.

"How many minutes till they change the guard?" A silence as one of the men dug through pockets, searching for a watch. I imagined I could hear the ticking of the second hand from down here in my pit, beneath the sheltering limbs of a great, wide fir tree.

"Seventeen." That was a different voice. Dong E started the moment the other man, the third man, spoke.

"Down here!" she called out. "Menghai! We're down here!"

The men on the road above us, seemingly just as surprised by Dong E's outburst as I was, started and looked around in every direction, aiming their rifles foolishly into the blackened forest. Dong E began to scramble and her efforts brought the walls of our hiding spot down around us. Snow piled on my head, slipped beneath the tangled layers of my spoiled clothes and chilled me to the bone as if I had been thrown into an icy lake. Without hesitating, I scampered up the bank behind Dong E and, after much exertion, and a couple times sliding back down to the bottom, I succeeded in grabbing the hand offered by one of the men who had happened upon us. When he pulled me up to the road and threw a cloak over my shivering frame, I looked at the three men and saw a trio of warriors staring back at me with dull eyes that seemed to swallow all the residual moonlight that had filtered through the canopy. They were silent. Standing before the man who had pulled me out, I realized that he was Zheng Menghai, the food porter, who had never bowed to the Japanese commissary man. I trembled in the night shadow of his mountainous frame. He held a carbine rifle in his hand and his parka was cinched tight against the snow, but I knew it was him. I could sense it. The other men had slight postures and were doubled over from the exertion from walking through the deep snow all the way from the village, but Zheng Menghai towered above us all. The men all carried rifles and pistols as well. The one furthest away from me, who seemed to be the smallest—no taller than a child—had a bulbous growth sticking out of his hips that looked awfully like a bundle of dynamite.

"How did you girls get this far wearing so little?" His first question. We stammered meaningless, contradictory words in the darkness that made no sense at all. We talked over each other and, in the end, said nothing at all. I tried to tell them about the escape but, every time I opened my mouth, images of days of torture would resurface and scare my words away.

"You should both be dead, right now, in this cold." Zheng said, his voice bearing the paternal worry of a father whose only just found his lost children. "This is not the night you should have left. What were you thinking?"

"We—we—" I began. "We couldn't. Not one more night."

In the silence, the men exchanged glances. Dong E interrupted their silent communication. "Are you on your way to attack it?" There were silent stares between the men again and then they all turned to look at Dong E at the same time. "Yes. But I suppose we can't any longer."

"Comrade!" said the small man, the one with the dynamite, "We need to! They are bleeding us dry and we won't live out the winter on what they leave for us."

"There will have to be a way. Tonight, we take these women to the farm. It's already late and they will be dead soon. Besides, the camp will be alert and waiting. They would not want to be fooled twice in one night."

Apparently, Zheng Menghai had the final word. When he said that they were rerouting to "the farm," wherever that was, the men ceased griping and immediately pulled out the maps, their compasses, shouldered their rifles, found their bearings, and began walking. They marched in single file and Zheng Menghai, walking behind us, ordered us to do the same.

"So the Japanese don't know how many we are if they find our tracks in the morning," he said, without necessarily addressing either one of us. He spoke to the trees and the owls looking down at us with mild curiosity. After we entered the forest, the men pulled limbs from dead trees and placed them in the way of our trail, obscuring the direction we were taking.

Though I still shivered with great, heaving motions that threatened to knock me off my balance, I felt consoled by the presence of comrades and, suddenly, I had the impression that my entire life in the pleasure camp was a dream, that instead of leaving my old village with Nainai, Wuxiao, and Xaio Si, I instead joined the Eighth Route Army and had been fighting the Japanese in secret ever since. It comforted me and kept me alert, this fantasy of mine, and as the cold continued to tighten its noose around me, I held it close.

After what seemed like many lis, the precipitous mountain slopes gave way to rolling meadows, and before long, the five of us came to a clearing—a great big field in the forest. The fields had turned to heather and bramble and the fences that still stood were choked with cadaverous remains of that summer's climbing vines and weeds that seemed to have had the run of the place for ages. The briar was so thick that our movement created a commotion and scattered the tittering field mice from their nests. I didn't even notice the neglected structure that sat at the center of it all. Its roof sported a slope that did not look entirely even or secure and, even in the night, I could tell that a big chunk of the chimney had fallen and crushed the garden beds beneath it. We approached the house and the men fanned out, forming a ring around the building and simultaneously entering from different doorways. Dong E and I exchanged nervous glances as the men cleared the cottage and, when their voices beckoned us into its safety, we took off running, eager to be out of the wind.

There were numerous blankets that we wrapped ourselves in and we covered the windows with the rest. Zheng Menghai built a small cook fire in the eave but would not let us build one in the fireplace. It was too dangerous, he said, and he would not hear any more of it. We contented ourselves to squeeze the fabric of our new, dry blankets close and huddle beside each other with longing in our eyes as we stared at the barren hearth.

When his cook fire grew hot enough, he put on tea and not long after, Dong E and I sipped slowly at the steaming water in our bowls and told the men everything we knew about the compound—its layout, the number of people who were inside, and where the weapons were. Even Dong E seemed surprised by my extensive knowledge of the layout and troop movements within the compound. I confessed my longing for her while she was imprisoned in the caves, and that I had nothing to do but watch the comings and the goings from the window of my cell. No one said anything and in the stillness, I found myself wishing I hadn't said anything at all.

But the moment passed and, before long, the tactical and militaristic conversation gave way to stories from the warfront, stories about the Eighth Route Army and

Mao's forces to the south. The Japanese were winning the war, Menghai said. There was no doubt about it. They had sacked all of the major coastal cities and the atrocities performed there would boil the blood of even a sage. They were winning but many still fought. They still hoped. They all knew that the root of communism would never be plucked from their garden by the Japanese imperialists. Listening to Zheng Menghai speak, I had the distinct impression that he would one day be a statesman, if ever this war ended. Though he would never look comfortable in a boxy, uncomfortable suit, his words and his melodious voice had a hypnotic lure that made me feel as if anything he said was destined to pass. He had that hold over people.

After he had finished telling us about the war, I asked him if he had ever heard of a man named Wuxiao Li of Yangquan. The men all looked at one another and a dreadful feeling washed over me. Their faces were paler than one caused by mere cold and I had a feeling that devastating news would arrive momentarily. They looked at one another, then back at me, and I could sense Dong E fidgeting in her seat beside me. "Tell me," I said, picking up on the obvious agitation my question had caused. "Just let it out, already!" Zheng Menghai stared straight into my eyes as he spoke: "He is back in Yangquan. He fought for a while but was injured. I believe he is still there."

The news, so different from what I had expected, knocked the air out of me. My eyes went wide, my fingers began to twitch with excitement. "Is Nainai alive?" I asked, "Xiao Si?" I was certain I would explode into dancing right there. The realization of my newfound freedom and the revelation that my husband was still alive hit me at the same moment and in that instant—how I wished I could have remained there permanently! What pain would have been avoided!—I felt that not even the entire Japanese army would prevent me from walking naked there through ten blizzards. For the rest of the night, I was ecstatic and driven and, suddenly, felt as if my life had a renewed purpose. The rest of them talked and I thought only about my impending reunion with my family. With Xiao Si, my old friend. That night, everyone slept soundly, and I stayed awake until the sun broached the cloud coverage in the early hours of the morning, listening to the chorus of snoring and nighttime grunts that washed over me like a tide.

"I have decided," Dong E said over tea the following morning, after everyone had begun to prepare for the day's march, "that I am staying with Zheng Menghai." She spoke the words with an air of melancholy and they saddened my ears to hear. I had not considered the parting of ways that would soon be upon us. I thought about Dong E in the pleasure camp and her steadfast will in the months before. She would also go on to great things, if the war ever ended, but I would not be a part of them. I knew that just as surely as she knew that her path remained intertwined with Menghai's. I sipped my tea, first dispersing the steam with a thin, placid jet of air from my pursed lips.

"I know. I know. This is where you belong." I put my tea down and faced her. "You are one of those special people, Dong E, who will always know the way. Some people have the talent, the magic within them, to lead others. You are one of them." She drew me into an embrace, and we said nothing more on the subject. As the men filed into the room, their winter garments bundled against their necks and their limbs were impeded by the many layers they wore. Talk switched to the direction they would take, and when their wagon would arrive.

"Is he even going to come at all?" one of them asked.

"And Zheng Menghai responded, "If I do not rendezvous with him, he will be here. That was the plan and Hai is a very reliable person."

"Then when's he going to get here? I'm getting anxious. The Japanese will be looking for these two."

"Any minute," said Zheng Menghai. As if to reaffirm his all knowing sage-like nature that had impressed me the night before, the lane to the cottage was disturbed a few moments later, and the rattling of a carriage and the clopping of donkey hooves slipping through the ice and snow filled our morning. It was time to leave.

The carriage was piloted by an old man who appeared blind, though this must have been a ruse to fool the Japanese. He commanded the carriage with deft precision and came to a stop with a soft noise that stopped his donkey in its tracks. The men all exchanged cheerful greetings with the old man but he looked at the two of us women with a wary glance, as if our sudden appearance in his plans were not a good omen.

They conferred and soon after they went into their huddle, Zheng Menghai called out to us and told us to climb underneath the boxes of yams where we would not be discovered. We did as we were told and, though I had a sinking feeling in the pit of my stomach that I could not properly diagnose as either nerves or fear or a sense of ill tidings, I felt a twinge of excitement at being on a journey once more, with comrades by my side. The darkness crowded in on us again when they stacked the boxes high over the secret compartment that Dong E and I had crawled into. The ride would be long and the cart bouncing. We were sandwiched together in the cramped space but I liked the feeling of her warmth at my side and I still strongly suspected that this would be the last memory we shared together. The groan of stressed wooden boards and the rickety turning of the wheels told us that our journey had begun.

Chapter 14

IT FELT LIKE TIME THAT WE spent huddled together beneath the boards of the wagon, jostled by every bump in the wagon trail, every rut, every pothole, would last forever. Every time we came to a halt, the muffled voices of our comrades would signal that we had been stopped by Japanese at checkpoints. In these moments, even a heartbeat seemed to echo like the cry of a raven over a great, wide canyon, and I would feel the sweat forming on Dong E's palms as I squeezed them in my own. The sound of shifting crates, the discussion of weary Japanese soldiers and weary Chinese merchants, crossing paths in the wild places between villages, chilled and terrified me and kept me feeling alive and a part of something, like I was a great warrior of the Eighth Route Army being smuggled to the next battlefront. These stops were the rhythm by which we timed our journey.

At some point, we came to a final stop. There were no Japanese voices and no shifting of crates. Only the dull quiet of men who know they are up to no good and work quickly and quietly to dispense with their duties as fast as possible. The boards were lifted and sunlight blasted into our dark recess. I recoiled from it, shielding my eyes from its blinding power and realized, not for the first time since the war started, that it had made nocturnal beasts of us. This war. Constantly hiding, burrowing into holes, rolling in ditches to cover ourselves with mud and gain the appearance of a corpse among the others so the Japanese might not see us. How many Chinese had to bear these hardships?

I rested easy at night knowing that I was not alone. It was a similar feeling to when I was arriving at Yangquan for the first time, not knowing the future. But those feelings of terror, of always being on the run, were dispelled when Zheng Menghai offered his hand to me and pulled me from the compartment. Though my joints ached with the effort, standing at my full height had never felt so good. Dong E cracked her back and stretched her muscles, reaching her arms up high above her head and releasing a pleasurable groan as her tendons and muscles finally released their pent up tension. It looked as if she were trying to fly away, to reach so high up that she would be able to grab a cloud and leave the world behind forever.

The men looked furtively everywhere and, following their lead, I took in my surroundings. We had stopped in a forest grove and, judging by the flickering lights that danced in the trees and the smell of roasted chicken and garlic that reached my nostril, we were just on the outskirts of Yangquan. I yearned for it. The life that I had begun in this village had seemed so dreary, so far removed from any seed of love when I had first arrived all those months ago. Wuxiao had seemed a weak child, undeserving of a wife, and his grandmother had inspired a great, deep fear in me that verged on outright hatred when she would scold me, deride my family's poverty, and talk to me as if she had personally done me a great favor by purchasing me like a shank of beef and breeding me with her grandson. But now, as the lights of the village flickered in the distance, I imagined the reunion, picturing the feast laid out, the warmth of an embrace, the feel of Wuxiao when we lay together. I am ashamed to admit that my heart began to flutter like that of an excited child when I imagined it. How stupid I was, then.

"We cannot linger long," Zheng Menghai said to me. "The Eighth Route Army needs supplies, and it is on me to supply them. We must be going." The party all looked at me; the somber tone that Zheng Menghai used when he spoke drove the fact home that this was a parting of ways. For all the horrors of war, it did bring me and Dong E together. My entire life had been spent thus far in the journeys of others, constantly being picked up and shipped to another corner of the country like a pumpkin in a sack. But in all of these travels, I had never experienced a true, meaningful parting of ways. The thought made me tear up. Dong E had the same tears in her eyes and her lips quivered when we made eye contact. We didn't say anything to each other—not at first. The powerful look in her eyes communicated enough and I felt her silent sobs reverberating through her arms as she locked me in an embrace that pushed all of the air out of my lungs. It felt like an eternity spent in her embrace and it would have suited me just fine, but I had my husband to find, my house to keep in order and, just as I was saddened to leave the party and Dong E behind, I was equally excited to put the war in the past and resume whatever remained of my life. They were waiting for me. When we broke our bear hug, she looked me in the eyes and they reflected the orange tamarind color of the sunset, and she whispered in my ear, "You deserve this. I won't forget you." "Nor could I forget you, Dong E," I said, and the words felt clunky and awkward as they came out of my mouth. I felt like a child for the second time since climbing out of the wagon's hidden recess.

Suddenly there was nothing left to say and the bitter cold of winter cut through the stillness of the grove. I shivered and so did Dong E. The men called to her and she turned away from me. She spared a last glance as she was crawling back into the cubby and called out just as the boards were being replaced, "Hey! Without you breathing all the air, this is pretty nice!" She chuckled and I gave a forced smile that I feared would turn into sobs if they did not set out soon. When they had the cart loaded up again, they climbed into the back and the donkey began to clop its way down the path. The men waved at me and Zheng Menghai's shoulders remained in view until the forest swallowed up even his hulking frame, leaving me alone with nothing but the lonely call of a disinterested owl echoing through the trees. I turned my back on the grove then and set out for Yangquan on foot. My family was waiting. My life was waiting. I was so positive that it would be exactly as I remembered it, that everything would be as if nothing had happened in the first place.

#

This was not the case, and I noticed immediately upon my arrival in the town that the war had hardened the people here. The men who had not left for the war were all broken and crippled and sat in their doorsteps giving everything that moved a glare that would turn your hair white. The women hunched over cook fires were all haggard and bent at the waist like the gnarled trunks of ancient trees and they stared at me with the same look as I shuffled past, through the main lanes and over to the outskirts. They all seemed strangers to me and, with a somber realization, I figured that they were. The war had changed everything and I wasn't here. I wasn't a part of this village anymore.

When I saw the old home, I thought my feelings would be dispelled, but they were only compounded. Despite the bitter cold, no smoke wafted from the chimney. The barren trees in the adjacent orchards had not been pruned the previous year and looked like the skeletal hands of a corpse protruding from the soil. I proceeded cautiously up the lane, suddenly feeling uneasy about the whole venture and sincerely wishing I had chosen to stay with Dong E and Zheng Menghai.

But I had not and now I was here, again, standing before the same doors I had encountered so long ago, feeling much the same sense of displacement that had gripped me then. The house seemed empty but I knocked anyway. After a long pause, the knob turned, squealing in protest as the tumblers ground against the rusty mechanisms of the latch. With a shudder, the door was wrenched open and I saw a face that at first did not seem familiar. An old man, wispy beard cascading from a pointed chin and his eyes narrowed as if he had spent far too much time farming his fields and squinting against the sun. His shoulders were slumped and his otherwise warm smile was tarnished by the black stains that marred his teeth. His eyes were the picture of happiness, and he threw his arms as high above his shoulders as he could manage and exclaimed that his wait was over. He beckoned me inside, but I felt a moment of hesitation and confusion that I knew was written all over my face.

"Excuse me," I said, from the doorstep. "Is this not the house of Wuxiao Li?" He laughed, his joy uncontainable. "Come in, my darling. I have water boiling for tea and soup on the hearth. It is meager but there are beans in it!" He laughed at that, as if he had said something extraordinarily funny, and my perplexity only grew. I did, however, walk in after him. The familiar home was distorted by unfamiliar scents and the arrangement of the furniture was different from how I remembered. It seemed as if everything in the home was cast in a grim pallor, as if the colors had faded from the very walls. The whole time, he explained to me what had happened to

Wuxiao and my exasperation at his every word seemed not to register. He was overjoyed.

"The Lis's sold the place to my son. They were destitute. I do not know what happened to them?" I pressed them for more information, fearing that rather than my journey ending at this dreary doorstep, it was only just beginning. "Where did they go? Is Nainai alive?" I pestered him with more and more questions as he fixed tea, trying to figure out, if nothing else, in what direction they had wandered. Apparently, they were broken by the war and reduced to shadows of their former selves. When I asked about Xiao Si, the man only shrugged his shoulders and said something about joining the National Revolutionary Army. She was probably dead now he said with a chuckle. His irreverence disturbed me even more than the agile range of motion that belied his incredible age.

Finally, with no interlude whatsoever, he asked a question of me. "Why do you care about those people anyway?" he said, "They sold you, too." The man with the blackened, crooked teeth and the shoulders like sloping hills in an endless meadow delivered the news with a smile on his face and a cup of lotus flower tea extended in a chipped wooden goblet. He seemed to be on the other side of a great valley. His words barely reached my ears, and I started panting as the room began to spin. I staggered backwards, and when I dropped the tea that he offered me, he gave another one of his patent chuckles that I would come to loathe and then admire.

"Silly girl," he said. "Not to worry though, an easy spill, that one. I'll go get the rags."

And just like that, he disappeared into the kitchen again, leaving me alone with my thoughts. They raged in my head like a great storm and, for the first time since leaving the pleasure camp, I missed the howl of the lonely wind on the mountaintop at nights. I imagined the transaction—Nainai and her cold, austere calculation, counting coins with her spidery fingers—and felt a seething hatred, a sense of betrayal, and a fear of the unknown rising up inside me to contend with one another. I spotted a rug on the floor that looked familiar. I lowered myself onto it and brought my knees close to my chest. My whole body shook with rage, shame, and humiliation. The whole time, the old man, who told me from around the corner that his name was Li Jigui, continued his prattling, though his words scarcely made an impression on me. "They told me about your... situation... and I want to clear the air right now, it doesn't matter to me." He punctuated his statement of benevolence with the sickening chuckle again and my spine shivered. "I'll care for you just the same. You are my wife."

He came back into the room and mopped up the spilt tea and handed me a bowl of soup with a joke about not spilling it, but it all happened so fast. I was unable to keep up with it and suddenly felt a burning sensation of loss at the memory of Dong E crawling back into the cubby beneath the floorboards of the wagon outside of town. How I would have loved to be crammed in there with her right now; what a horrible mistake I had made. It all sunk in.

Li Jigui, for his part, realized my discomfit and sat beside me. He did not nestle against me or try to drape his bony arm across my shoulders and, for that, I was grateful. Truly. I would have broken his arm if he touched me in that moment. "They gave me no small amount of silver for you," he said with a somber air and his giddiness finally subsided. He did not laugh at the end of this statement, but looked bashfully at the floor in front of us. "They must have valued you." The words sounded so wrong, so empty, but I could not deny the warmth that Li Jigui conveyed through speaking them. His voice had a melodious air, like that of a man who had seen the entire world, and remembered every bit of it. Like a poet, well versed in speaking aloud. Or a lonely man, who had no one to talk to but himself and was glad to finally have the company of another. "In any case," he said as I sat in my catatonic stupor, "You can sleep in the bedroom tonight. I know this must be hard for you. I don't mind sleeping out here."

He helped me to my feet and led me gingerly to the bedroom, where I was left in solace and silence. As I lay on the stove kang and stared out the only window the room offered, I had memories of Nainai rushing over me, overcoming my consciousness. I remembered when I carried her on my back up the mountain passes and stayed with her while the Japanese were circling us. I remembered the terror that overcame me when I watched the soldiers kicking and beating her. I remembered the look of pity she gave me when I first arrived at her doorstep. And I hated her. Every terrible thing that had befallen me in the past year was of her making and my heart accelerated as I basked in the hatred that took over every centimeter of my body. But the fatigue of the journey and the comforts of the kang overcame my hatred and feelings of betrayal and, before long, I drifted off to sleep.

I was shaken awake the next morning by my new husband, who held in his palsied hands another cup of lotus blossom tea that filled the room with its aroma. The sun slanted in through the window, and the sound of naked branches scraping against each other in the gentle breeze outside was like the soothing sounds of an ocean lapping incessantly at the shores.

"Drink up, dear," he said. "You have a long day ahead of you." I looked at him with puzzlement but said nothing. He seemed to sense a question in my stare, and answered willingly enough. "Oh yes. I got in touch with the doctor, and he should be by to help your wounds heal. He's not the best, but he is the only doctor we have."

I took his offered tea and sipped gingerly at it, feeling the warmth rejuvenating me. How long had it been since I had a proper cup of tea? I didn't even want to think about it.

I stood up and readied myself for the day. It was a strange sensation, being free to walk about and prepare for a day whose activities would be of my own choosing. I do not think I experienced that freedom since my childhood and it produced an empty feeling in me, as if I could not come up with anything to fill the hours as we waited for the doctor to arrive. I sat with Li Jigui and he told me all about his own experiences with the war. The soldiers occupying the village, the forced migrations, the murders he had seen committed. He watched the soldiers pull a child out of his mother's arms and stab him to death with bayonets. He watched them throw grenades into homes with mothers cowering over their children. He wondered how he even survived at all, and when the room fell silent, we talked about the weather.

On that first day of our life together, we had already adopted the habits of a long-married couple. After exchanging awkward small talk, he left me to my business and I left him to his. The only problem was that, after so many months of captivity, I did not know what my business entailed. I did not know anything anymore, except the feel of Japanese dogs inside me and the hatred that the feeling inspired. But in the solitude in which I found myself, I realized that it could be much worse. Though his teeth were rotting and his back hunched, he had a warm smile, and he used the money that he had received to pay for a doctor. Perhaps this would not be as terrible as I figured at first, but the steel grey sky that lingered overhead reminded me that, in the end, the world did not care about me and that I was on my own. For now, I would try to enjoy my time with my new husband, at least as long as I could manage.

Chapter 15

THE FIRST DAYS OF MY marriage to Li Jigui passed with me healing, him working, and the doctor's frequent visits becoming the means by which we marked the passage of time. Despite the condition of the town and the broken spirits of those who remained here, these days were easy for me. Li Jigui was a gentleman the whole time and never made any undue efforts to strip me naked or throw me on the kang when the sun went down. He made tea, he cooked the food, and he went to the markets to sell whatever we could in order to pay for my treatments. The house—once the domicile of Nainai and my old husband, was growing more and more empty with every passing day and everything that we did not burn for warmth was brought into the village and sold to whomever would be willing to buy. In this manner, we made our living. My elbows and knees began to function properly and, by the time the spring blossomed and brought a touch of warmth to our valley, I was walking perfectly fine and even planting tubers in the garden beds that lined our property.

The Eighth Route Army was further away than they ever had been before and news of their fight was increasingly rare. Every time I heard someone mention the war effort, I thought about Zheng Menghai and Dong E and wondered if they were still alive, if they were okay, if they had food to eat, or if they were scrounging in strangers' larders for a morsel. But their faces were blurry in my memories, as if they were characters from a story not my own and, despite the love that I still felt for them, I enjoyed the distance that the war had put between itself and my own life. My new husband and I were almost able to pretend that there was no war. When that fantasy would begin to take hold, however, a stray soldier would wander into the village, bloodied and dying, or a bomb would detonate in the hills, vibrating the few glass windows that remained in the village, and the illusion would be shattered.

Still, though, we were happy. The tubers came in nice, the harvest was fruitful, and smiles began to surface on the war weary faces of the villagers, who no longer looked like refugees, but who had, instead, settled down and begun to live post-war lives. I kept thinking that at any moment, the Japanese would fall upon us and the whole nightmare would begin anew, that we would be chased from the village or shot with our backs against the walls of our home, but each day that dawned and passed without event dulled the expectation with which I waited for the tribulations to begin again.

By the end of that summer, when the fall set in—not nearly so cold as the previous autumn—I scarcely thought about the war at all, except late at night, when I would wake from a dream with the faces of Xinyi Sung and Dong E and Xiao Si still lingering. Those nights, it was hard to tell the difference between the pleasure camp and my home, and I would wake with a shout that startled Li Jigui from his own dreams. But he never complained. No matter what happened in our daily life, it seemed he always had his signature smile, and gave his signature chuckle after every statement, as if nothing perturbed him, as if the war had never happened. It was refreshing. Fall gave way to winter, but we had food. Winter bled into spring and summer arrived shortly after. The Japanese were nowhere.

I told myself not to be too happy about this. Not to fall into the lull of forgetfulness until every Japanese dog was safely back in their own country, far away from us. But as the days continued to pass with no events, it became increasingly hard to remind myself that war was still imminent and that any day could be the one the Japanese decided that our village served some arcane and useful purpose for their war efforts. We spent many years in this manner.

\#

In the summer of 1943, the world had forgotten about us lowly peasants in the mountains. I had never been happier. The watermelons were coming in ripe and succulent and we, in Yangquan, had great festivals to celebrate our good fortune. Whole pigs were roasted on spits and the chickens gave us bountiful piles of eggs that we turned into all manner of delicacies and sweets and soups. We walked through the fair and absorbed the scents of meat cooking, the sounds of children laughing, the warmth of the sun gracing our cheeks and foreheads and shoulders as it shone down upon us. After a morning of walking through the village together, we parted ways. Li Jigui went to the house and I to the fields. We had our own vines of ripe watermelons that needed to be plucked and harvested and organized in the larder. He needed to find someone to buy them. The valley had been so bountiful that summer that scarcely anyone wanted for food, and my husband busied himself trying to find people in other villages who would buy our fruits or barter for them with fuel or clothing or anything else useful to us. Just because the war had forsaken our valley, did not mean that the supplies we needed were once again easy to find.

That is how I came to be separated from Li Jigui and, to this day, I remember the sound of his chuckle and the smile upon his face when he called out to me, just down the lane a little bit. "You be careful now. Don't throw out your back with all those watermelons or we will not be able to keep harvesting!" He laughed, as he always did, and I returned his laughter with a sincere smile of my own. We parted ways, and I never saw him again.

The fields where we had planted our watermelons ran adjacent to the main road that led into Yangquan Village and offered views of the road that would allow anyone to see approaching carts or vehicles or pedestrians. The foliage, though dense, did not completely cover the road and, in the deepest moments of paranoia a few years before, when I would be sure that Japanese were going to fall upon the village at any moment, I would anxiously keep watch in that field, so I would know first if the Japanese dogs were actually coming for us. But I did not see them. Maybe I was too busy with my melons to catch them sneaking through the underbrush and crawling through the mud with their camouflage uniforms and their rifles slung over their shoulders. Maybe I did see them, but just could not admit to myself that the pleasurable days of a war that was not at my doorstep were coming to an abrupt end.

I heard the women shouting before I noticed anything else. The sound was blood curdling and the shrieks echoed through the still summer air and scattered a small group of roosting birds from their perches. I turned immediately to the sound of the shouts and saw my neighbors running toward me with their clothes billowing after them, their arms flailing, and their voices raised to the sky in anger, fear, and alarm. "They are here!" one of the women shouted as she turned her knees high above the watermelons vines and pumped her fists with the exertion of her sprint. "Everyone hide! The Japanese are here!"

I did not need a second warning. The woman who had been screaming was tackled by a soldier who had been closely pursuing her, and her body hit the vines with an audible grunt of pain and resignation. My heart began to slam against my ribs and before I even realized what I was doing, my body had completely taken over, and I found myself running toward my house. The other women who were closer to the road were also tackled and, every time I looked over my shoulders, I saw more Japanese sneaking from the ditches along the side of the road. I needed to get inside. I needed to hide. That is what one part of my mind told me and its voice was clear and calm in my head, despite the horrid scenes playing out around me.

By now, jeeps had torn up the road leading into town and the staccato rapping of mounted machine gun fire echoed through the day and shattered whatever remained of the stillness that I had been enjoying so much. I kept thinking about Li Jigui and what he had told me to do in the event that the Japanese ever came back to Yangquan.

There are loose boards in the ladder. If you need to, it should take only a second to climb in and replace the boards. And there is food down there if you must wait.

His voice sounded so clear in my head but so, too, did another voice—that of Dong E—imploring me to grab Li Jigui's single shot hunting rifle and the bag of shells that he kept in the house. It was Dong E who I listened to. When I made it into the house, my hands shook with nerves and excitement but I found the rifle, exactly where I knew it would be, and the shells right next to it. From where I stood, I could see the field that I had just run through. It was crawling with Japanese soldiers and the man in the lead had insignias and braided ropes hanging from his uniform everywhere. A man of importance. With my trembling fingers, I somehow managed to slide a cartridge into the breach-loader and clicked the gun shut with an audible sound that reminded me of a heavy, iron lock slamming shut on a prison door.

I ran to the porch. The soldiers who were chasing me had nearly made it to the fence and were moving quickly, cutting back and forth in a zigzag pattern to make shooting almost impossible. But the voice of Dong E steadied my hand, echoing through my mind and bringing back to the long forgotten day all those years ago, when I and Xiao Si and the Wuxiao had attended her talk about how to properly use firearms against soldiers.

You must hold your breath, slacken your shoulders, and gently squeeze.

I followed her instructions and the blast of gun smoke and cordite that erupted from the muzzle almost knocked me to the ground. It blinded me as the smoke stung my eyes and tears of rage formed along my lashes. But when I squinted and wiped away the tears from my eyes, I saw the leader of the soldiers clutching at his belly with a stupefied look on his face, as if he could not imagine that he had just been shot dead by a Chinese woman. The others had fallen to the ground and drew their own rifles and, while I struggled to open up the gun and get another round in the chamber, the porch splintered and erupted in a shower of wood chips that stuck in my hair, pierced my skin, and sent me running back into the house.

I managed to reload, though, and got one more shot off. Another soldier fell, this time from a bullet through his thigh. His scream of pain sounded like the screams Dong E and Xinyi Sung had to muster when the dogs were upon us at the pleasure camp and hearing that sound from the mouth of a Japanese soldier brought a smile to my face. I changed my position again, just as Dong E had taught and got a third shot off, but it went wild. Now, as I scanned the property line, I saw the ring forming around my position and knew that it was going to be a fight to the death. Shots four and five found their home in the torsos of soldiers, who crumpled like paper dolls.

But when I loaded the sixth shot and leveled the rifle at the oncoming soldiers, I felt, out of nowhere, the stinging yet somehow dull pain that covered my entire body, and the world turned itself upside down and went black. I felt the force of a great and powerful blow against the side of my head and, when I turned in that direction, I saw a crazed soldier with blood running down his face and neck baring his teeth at me. I lashed out with my feet, kicking him in the groin and watching him double over with a groan of agony. Jumping to my feet, I kicked him again and wrestled the pistol from his holster. I levelled it at his head, and saw in his face the same look of surprised terror that had been written all over Xinyi just before her death. It is funny the memories that surface in your mind when you have a gun aimed at someone's head and are ready to pull the trigger.

But I never did pull the trigger. I hesitated for only the slightest moment and, before my finger tightened its grip, I felt a hand grab at my hair and, before I could react, I was pulled to the ground and showered with blows on every part of my body. I curled up into a ball, tried to protect my ribs, but when a steel boot crashed into them, the crunch of their breaking shattered my resolve, and I blacked out as the soldiers dragged me from the kitchen and onto the porch. They continued to beat me there and everything went black as my gaze drifted off toward the sky.

I woke up in the back of a truck, bound at the wrists and ankles and huddled together amid the smell of sweat and gasoline and the smoke of fires that drifted over from the village. I blinked and even that movement caused an immense explosion of pain that sent me back into unconsciousness.

I came out of my swoon for a second time when the truck lurched forward and the sound of its engine backfiring cracked the shell of my convoluted and twisted dreams. I scanned the faces around me and saw the same look of confusion and terror on every single one. Almost every young woman from the village was in that truck and we all groaned and moaned with pain as the truck rocked and bounced on the pothole strewn path that led away from the village. Looking around for a second time, not a single man was in the back of the truck with us.

That is when I knew the terrors that awaited us. That is when I knew where the truck was going and, in a desperate frenzy, fought against the ropes that bound my limbs together but had to give up when the pain became too great. The pleasure camp. Did any of these women know what lay in store for them? Did anyone have these memories to keep down, besides me? I thought that I should tell everyone, that I should scream as loudly as I could and convince all of the women to rise up, that bullets would be better than what awaited us. But when I saw the terrified faces of the children who huddled against their mother's bosoms, I could not bring myself to add to their torment. Besides, even breath created an unbearable pain that originated at my chest and reached even the extremities of my toes and fingers. No. Better to sleep. Better to save my energy.

I had escaped once, and was sure that I could do it again, but I would need my energy and my strength and I would need to be in shape for running through the woods again. If I created a scene, the soldiers would stop the truck right there, march me to the drainage ditches that lined the sides of the road, and put a bullet in my head. They would leave my corpse in the ditch, and it would stay there until I rotted into nothingness. I asked myself which fate was worse and I could not decide. The rocking of the vehicle created explosions of pain and I found myself thinking about Li Jigui and the watermelons, and the festival that the Japanese had ruined. Would it ever end? I did not think so. But I did not want to give up either. Perhaps some vestige of the strength that Dong E had imparted to me still lingered because every time the pain spread from my broken bones, I stolidly bore it and made not a sound. No, I would not give in. I would not let the Japanese win nor would I become another broken woman at the hands of their abuse.

The truck climbed slowly up the mountain passes and the women on all sides of me asked in hushed voices where we were going, what they were doing to us. I knew the answers. An older woman said that the soldiers were bringing us to a prisoners' camp and would turn us over to the Chinese authorities because we were not soldiers. It was a soothing fantasy that I would not shatter for the other women. I could not. Rather, I let the rolling of the wheels and the monotonous hum of the diesel engines lull me back into a state of unconsciousness. I needed to save energy. I needed to be ready to fight when the opportunity arose.

When I saw the tall walls of the pleasure camp looming around the last bend, my heart sank, but I also had the strange feeling of returning to a place that I had once called home. It looked exactly as I remembered it and, when they unloaded us from the back of the truck and marched us past the locust tree that I had once been tied to, I noticed that the red stains where they tied women up were so much darker than they had been, and I was sure that this was not a trick of the light or of my memories. Times were about to change and I was once more forced into the war.

Chapter 16

UNLIKE THE LAST TIME I was sent to this pleasure camp, this time I did keep track of the days. This time, I did scratch little marks into the cave walls and into the walls of the cells they locked us in in the fort. Ninety-three days, I spent there. Ninety-three days of being raped every night, beaten every day, and humiliated verbally throughout the entire experience. By now, my emotions were in tatters and I scarcely registered the pain I felt between my legs when a soldier would enter me. I had no virtue left to lose, no shame left to feel. It did not matter. Those were the darkest days of my life, and I think I can say the same for the soldiers, if their animalistic thrusting and their unpalatable groans were any measure to go by. Their faces melted into one uniform face, all grimaces and scars and war wounds. Their language, which was becoming familiar to me, was one unbroken slur against me and my people. But this inspired no hatred in me. I was far beyond feeling hatred. I think I was beyond feeling anything at all.

One night, a group of soldiers came into my room and all had their way, taking turns and beating me down and laughing all the while. At the end, they ripped my earrings out, and the blood that ran from the wound warmed my flesh and reminded me that this was no terrible dream. This was reality, and it would continue as it always did. The only thing I knew was that I would once again break free, that I would once again start a new life. That this, too, would one day pass, and my horrors would be at an end. I did not consider even once that they would execute me the way they did so many of my comrades in the camp. They would march us out in the warmth of the fading summer and stand us in a row, just as they had done when they murdered Xinyi Sung those many years ago. They would shout at us in their broken Mandarin and tell us about the victim's crimes. This one stole food, this one slapped a Japanese officer, this one did not moan loud enough for the soldiers who were raping her.

Then they would warn us of the fate that awaited each and every one of us if we did not fall into line, and then would shoot the woman who had been chosen as an example that week. I don't even know how many executions I had witnessed, how many bodies were thrown in the frozen river. As I counted off the days, I knew that winter was drawing closer and that, if I did not escape soon enough, I would have to wait until the spring to take the chance. It was only dumb luck that saved me and Dong E. If we had not stumbled upon Zheng Menghai, we would certainly have frozen to death out there in the forest and I was not planning on being that lucky for a second time. Why would I? I had experienced only death, rape, and destruction for my entire life and, in such times, one's life was only saved by a passing stranger but once. We Chinese were a damned race. No, the only hope of getting out of this hell would be to make my move before the first frost. I was positive that I would not be able to make it through another winter. I could not.

One day I noticed that a strange calm had fallen over the camp. No matter what time of day it was or what the soldiers were otherwise occupied with, the sound of rape and the humiliation of my comrades always reached my ears. It was as incessant as the howling wind that never let up on this accursed mountaintop. But on this day—I had lost track by this point, but I knew that summer was over and that fall had set in—the sounds were gone and the camp bore an awkward portentous stillness that I knew must have meant that the soldiers had left to go on a patrol or to gather more sex slaves or, in some other way, went to brutalize my countrymen. I did not know where they were or what they were doing or when they would be back. But as I sat in my cell and listened to the utter and complete silence that had fallen over the fortress like a light mist infiltrating a field in the earliest hours of dawn, I knew for certain that the soldiers—at least the vast majority of them—had gone elsewhere. I also knew that this would be my last chance to make an escape.

Frantically, I worked on the door latch with my fingernails. It was bolted shut from the outside, as it always was unless a soldier was enjoying me. No matter how hard I flung myself at the wooden frame, it would not budge. Despite hanging every ounce of my body weight on it, the door was immovable, solid. A wall, more than anything. As I continued to pull and push and pull and push and throw my body against it, it would not move the slightest bit, and a great panic sank its fangs into the calm resolve that had arisen in me when I realized the soldiers were gone.

No no no no no no no no no... My mind could not form any other words. Giving up on brute force, I scanned my surroundings for anything that would help. There were no loose floorboards. No blanket from a legendary revolutionary soldier. No, I had nothing at all except my two hands and my mind. Still, though, my efforts were not derailed. The mostly empty room had nothing in it but bars across the windows and a mat upon which the Japanese would throw me before they dropped their pants. There was nothing else. When the Japanese were conceiving this horrid camp, they had not forgotten anything at all. What could I use? Would I be able to pry up a floorboard, split it somehow, use my finger to pick the lock? That plan seemed so outlandish; just the fact that it had occurred to me for a moment made my situation seem so much more desperate. But what else was there?

I looked from one corner of the room to the other, trying to focus my mental energy. I walked over to the metal bars and tried to pry them, even going so far as to place my feet against the wall and, using the full force of my leg muscles, push against the wall and try to expose any concealed weakness in the bars. But it did not work. By the time I finished pulling the bars, I was sucking in big gasps of air that pushed my heart to the breaking point. Beads of sweat formed on my forehead and rolled down the curving arc of my cheekbones and down to my jaw. I almost gave up entirely and felt a wave of panic surging through me as I sat in the corner and tried to catch my breath. If I did not get this door open as soon as possible, the soldiers would come back to the camp and my hope of escaping would be dashed for the rest of the winter.

As I sat in the corner of the room with my head resting in the palms of my hands and my fingers bunching up my frayed hair, I noticed that one of the floorboards that I sat upon had a loose nail. The head of it stuck up only a dozen millimeters and it was barely noticeable. But to me, it was like a buoy in the middle of the ocean, a beacon in the night. I fell upon it with my fingernails, and when they began to chip and break, I lowered my face to the floor and latched onto the last vestige of hope with my own teeth. The pain rocketed from my teeth to my toes but I felt the nail rise up, if only the slightest bit. When it rose up enough to slip some fibers underneath it, I ripped a piece of my clothes, wrapped it around the nail's head until I could not fit another millimeter of cloth beneath the nail head and the floor, and then wrapped my finger around the fiber that still remained.

It broke, but not before loosening the nail about a centimeter. Now, I could fit my fingertips underneath it. I put all of my strength into the motion and rocked back and forth as I clung to the nail head, feeling it begin to slide up. When it finally gave, I was flung backward and slammed against the wall, my head bouncing off the supple boards. A slight trickle of blood coagulated in my hair but I did not care. I smiled and held the loose, bent nail close to the window. It was the perfect size.

I walked over to the door and inserted it into the lock. Jiggling it back and forth, back and forth, I tried to feel for the tumblers of the lock and felt a small jolt of exaltation every time I felt one of them giving way. When the last tumbler clicked into place and I felt the resistance of the doorknob dissipate, my heart flooded with warmth and a tingling sensation ran from my fingertips to my toes and back to my fingertips. My hands were shaking. My breathing came in fitful heaves that were arrhythmic and my ribs ached where the breaks had scarcely healed. But the door swung open and when I cautiously poked my head into the hallway, I saw exactly what I was hoping to see. Nothing at all. No soldiers, no commandant, no servants sweeping the corridors or refilling the vases that rested on the end tables and armoires. Nothing but a silent, empty fortress.

I crept through the halls, trying to remain quiet. I knew that not all the soldiers would have left. They certainly would have left some attachment behind to guard the fort. Then the thought struck me. Maybe they were in some cataclysmic firefight with the Eighth Route Army. Maybe they needed all the reinforcements they could muster, and pleasure camps be damned. I held out hope for this, thinking that Zheng Menghai and his revolutionary comrades might have saved me for a second time, and began to run through the halls, not caring that my feet created a slapping sound against the wooden boards. Not caring who might have heard.

All I knew was that not a single soul stood between me and the gate out of this place. I sprinted for the main doors of the fortress and threw them open. Light blinded me and I threw my arms over my eyes to shield them. The smell of rotting leaves and dead foliage washed over me and I felt a sense of rejuvenation as the autumn air, too, washed over me. I scanned the walls and found no soldiers there. I did not think twice about which direction to take; my legs pumping and my heart pounding, I ran for the gate and found it unlocked. For the second time, I threw my body into the wilderness and trusted in the trees to shelter me, the wolves to walk lithely past. It happened so fast that I did not even think for a second about consequences or the women in their own respective cells. I only thought that thirty minutes earlier, another Japanese soldier had his prick inside me and was laughing as he slugged a bottle of sake that he must have stolen from the mess. I thought that Li Jigui was waiting for me, that I knew the way back to Yangquan, that I could be there before the next sunrise.

Below this torrent of thoughts that raged continuously over the course of my flight through the woods, I knew that, just as easily as I could find the way, I could not safely return to Yangquan Village. What if the soldiers were there already? What if that is where they had gone? As I crashed through the trees and the branches and the brambles, I wondered where I should go. I knew that the logging road would be up ahead, that heading south on it would lead me back to Yangquan Village, but I was not entirely sure that it was the best course of action.

I thought then, for the first time since the war had begun, of the village of Xilianggou. I had passed through there during the years in which I had been traded from one family to another, one old crone to the next, each one in turn raising the price of marriage that had been attached to me. I had people there. It would be a long trek but I was sure that I could make it. When I found the logging road, instead of turning south toward Yangquan Village, I made my way north, into the forgotten wildernesses that made Yangquan Village look like a thriving metropolis.

In my head, I crunched numbers, wondering how long it would take, how many lis, how many steps, how many hours. I could not even begin to answer these questions, and the hunger that had taken hold of me during my flight from the camp would not let up, even after I began chewing on the bark of the fir trees that lined my path. I figured it would take me three days, that I had no idea whether or not my people were still there, and that I had no food to help me along the way. No known places to hide. It would be nearly impossible. I also knew that it was the only option that I had and, since I would be missing and my door would be found pried open upon the soldiers return, they would undoubtedly search through Yangquan looking for me. Therefore, I could not return.

Suddenly, with the aroma of conifers lingering in the fall air and the sound of migrating birds calling out to their kin, I thought about Yangquan and the girls still locked away in the camp. What would become of them? How would the Japanese torture them to exact their vengeance upon me? To dissuade any girls from following in my footsteps? These thoughts shook me and nearly stopped me in my tracks. Honestly, I thought about turning around, following my path of broken tree limbs back to the camp, walking through the same door I had just burst through, and locking myself back in the cell, just to save all the other girls from the retribution of the Japanese. But I could not. No way. I was breathing free air again and I was not going back. As if an impulse or an instinct was in charge of my mind, I continued to press forth, despite the horrifying images that continuously arose in my mind. I pushed them out. All the negative thoughts. Everything in my head that would entice me to give up.

I put one foot in front of the other and I watched the scenery change as I beat my own path to Xilianggou village, not once thinking that perhaps the Japanese soldiers would find me on this road. Not once thinking that the people I knew a long time ago in that village would perhaps not even be there or, even worse, not remember me when I came banging on their door seeking food and shelter and comfort. What would I do in that situation? I did not know what I would do. I had more questions than answers, and I felt a vague sense of terror blossoming in the pit of my stomach and spreading, but I did not want to acknowledge it.

The sun set and I was left in the darkness. I wanted a fire so badly but could not muster the courage to build one in the wild where the Japanese might be waiting for me. Instead, I slept in a ditch, huddled under heaps of moss and ferns and the detritus of fall season that piled up everywhere. I did the same thing the next night and the night after that and the night after that. I did that every night until a lingering fear gripped my mind and convinced me that I had been drastically mistaken in my judgements of distance and of the direction in which Xilianggou lay. I continued to nibble on dead leaves and sticks and pieces of bark and continued to think about how mistaken I was.

On the fifth day, though, I saw houses and smoke from the fires. I saw carts and heard the sounds of a market and I knew that after so many nights of uncertainty, I had found the village—or at least, a village. It could have been any village—friend or enemy. It could have been a Japanese base. I was so hungry, so terrified, so famished and out of energy that I would have fallen upon it anyway and begged door to door for food until someone found it in their heart to spare me.

But it was not a Japanese base. It was Xilianggou Village and, for the first time in months, I felt true happiness welling up within me. Though I knew enough at this point to keep the sensation of happiness in check, I thought that perhaps I was in luck, and that, this time, I actually would be safe. I walked with my head up, heading for the village, trying not to seem too weak. But hunger ate at me, and I knew I could not keep up the charade for long. The smell of herbs and roasting meat greeted my nostrils and I followed it into the village.

Chapter 17

THE VILLAGE HAD A SENSE of familiarity. Some roads were similar to how I remembered them as a child. Some, not so much. It was too cold at night for me to fall asleep, so I walked around, looking for food scraps left over by villagers. It looked as though food had been scarce here. Although it was not a war torn village such as Yangquan, it looked as if the war had robbed it of its potential. During the day, I slept under a tree at the entrance of the village. After two days of wandering and begging on the streets, Dr. Wu, an herbalist took pity on me. With peppered hair, Wu reminded me of Zheng Meng Tai who left with Dong E during our first escape from the pleasure camp. I had a familiar feeling toward him and I felt safe. He took me in as an assistant and also gave me some herbal treatment, given how rough I looked. He even fed me corn soup twice a day. It was much better than hunting for food scraps in the middle of the night for survival. As soon as my wounds started healing, I knew I could not be eating for free anymore; I needed to make myself useful. I picked up a broom and began sweeping the entryway of his shop. As I started feeling better, I started doing his laundry and delivering his herbs around the village. One night during dinner, Wu said, "I could use some help around my shop if you could stay around?"

"Of course. How can I ever repay you?"

As time went on, I moved from doing chores to getting trained in how to sort out herbal medicines when his patients needed them. Since the village was still poor, some of his patients could not afford to pay. He took payment in corn, pumpkins, flour, bread, and other items that we did not even need.

"We must get through this together," he said to me during dinner one time. I nodded in agreement, "At least we could make corn for dinner with their payment. There are starving people outside."

"I know, my family was starved to death during the famine," replied Wu. I had never heard about his family and had only imagined that he was living by himself because of choice. How much bitterness was there in reality?

I had been too ashamed to find my biological family. I heard rumors here and there about the death of my father and how my family fell apart. But I was too embarrassed to admit to anyone that I was their daughter. I decided to change my name in order to disguise who I was.

"Can I take your surname? Wu?" I asked Wu one night during dinner.

"Why? We are not married. It will give people the wrong impression," he replied stoically.

"It does not matter to me. I am not planning to get married since I cannot carry children anymore."

Wu nodded. "What do you think about the name Wu Lian Hua?"

"Lian Hua, as in lotus?" I asked.

"Yes, as a Buddhist saying goes, no mud, no lotus. And lotus are strong flowers that grow from mud."

I loved the name.

Although the war was over, it did considerable damage to, not only the village but, the whole country. Men who returned from the war were mostly crippled and more women turned to farm work and attending to household needs. More women were entering the workforce doing backbreaking work that men traditionally had done. The amount of work overwhelmed Wu and he decided to teach me basic acupuncture and massage techniques so I could handle the women's side of the clinic and divide our work evenly.

One day, a patient found a baby girl on the road. She was probably left there by desperate parents fleeing the war. The baby could not fend for herself and looked bewildered. Her eyes looked hopeless, as if she recently had been in a desperate situation. Our clinic was barely surviving and we could not feed another mouth, but maybe

I could make this one work. It would be hypocritical for me to sell her off as a child bride. What could possibly be her future? How could I be responsible for that? "I can just split my meals with her. She is small, we could share the same bed as well." I was trying to convince Wu about keeping the child. Wu thought about it for a while and finally agreed. "We need someone to eventually take over my herbal shop. Maybe this was heaven's way of answering that need. Why don't we name her Wu Min?"

And we never bound her feet.

One day, our family of three walked across a field ready to harvest. Farmers with baskets on their backs reminded me of my youth, picking crops, getting ready for another season. It felt as if I had lived multiple lifetimes throughout my life. I missed the field, the labor that brought us physical goods to trade, but I needed to look forward now. One day, when my child grew up, I would tell her all about what I had endured during the war. Maybe she will seek justice for not only me but also for Xinyi, Dong E and many other women who suffered through atrocities committed on many other Chinese people.

Interviews with Shanxi Comfort Women

Shanxi comfort station / pleasure camp where many women were captured, raped, and tortured.

The interviews below were conducted in 2014.

Tso Hei Mo

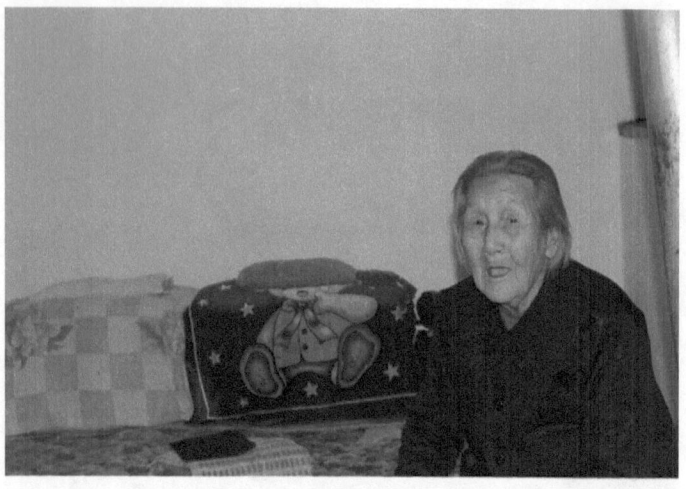

In the autumn of 1941, Japanese soldiers surrounded the entrance of her village and Tso Hei Mo was captured against her will. The Japanese soldiers kicked open the door of her home and dragged her out on the street. Then they raped her in front of all the villagers. At the time, she was already married. Like most at the time, she was a child bride. She was raped by multiple soldiers in the comfort station. Within the first year of her capture, she became pregnant and tried to get rid of it as soon as possible. She tried running around, lifting heavy objects, and even used her tummy to hit sharp edges of tables, and was able to lose the baby five months into her pregnancy. In the summer of 1943, she discovered that she was pregnant again. Due to that, fewer Japanese soldiers came to rape her at the cave. One night, her neighbor came and helped her to escape. It was not easy since she had bound feet. Her mother was embarrassed that she was carrying a Japanese baby, so they decided to give birth in a nearby cave and then abandoned the baby.

Hao Yuet Li

Hao was 15 when Japanese soldiers went to her house and kicked open the door while her parents were out working. Two soldiers rushed in with guns pointed at Hao who was terrified. While one soldier went to search for valuables, the other one took off her pants and raped her on top of the kang. After the first soldier raped her, the other one, who was searching for goods, took his turn and raped her. Then they took the valuables. Traumatized by this atrocity that happened in the morning, Hao hid under a blanket until the evening when the Japanese soldiers came back to her house and dragged her onto the main road. There she saw about ten Chinese men being chained to a rope and witnessed the Japanese soldiers waterboarding them. Along with two other girls, Hao was raped again. Soon, she started bleeding. Although, in exchange of money, she returned home after about a month, she was taken again two months later and gang raped day and night. She was starving and only allowed a bit to eat at night. Later, she was rescued by her father and brother. She could not even use the toilet when she got home. Up to this day, most of her expenses are her medical bills.

Zhuang Xian Tu

Zhuang Xian Tu was born in 1926 and married in 1941 to a 13-year-old boy when she was 16. On the morning of the second day of Chinese New Year in 1942, she was still celebrating the New Year and her recent marriage when some Japanese soldiers came to her house and took her. After looting her neighbors' houses, they came to her house. She was struggling with the soldiers to keep from being dragged out of the house. In the midst of struggle, one of the soldiers hit her legs and head with the back of his rifle. Her young husband begged the soldier not to take her, but the soldier threatened him with a bayonet and he was too scared to fight. Since she had bound feet, the soldiers grabbed her neighbor and made him carry her to the comfort station. The soldiers then took her, along with the village's food and her family's only donkey. The road to the comfort station was about 10 lis. If her neighbor walked too slowly on the journey, the soldiers beat him. Once they reached the destination, they were both exhausted. A Japanese soldier dragged her neighbor away and she was locked alone in a room where she was raped daily by countless soldiers. For more than 20 days she was locked up, punched and kicked when she did not comply with the soldiers' orders. Her face was slapped countless times in the period of time of her arrest. Guards at the door and around the comfort station prevented her from escaping. Her family sold valuables and borrowed from friends and relatives to buy her freedom. She was finally freed after violent treatment by the soldiers. She became ill but was not allowed treatment at her husband's household. People avoided her since she was considered a "dirty" woman for having satisfied soldiers at the comfort station. Suffering from illness and isolation at her in-laws, she decided to return to her father's house for a while to recover. She was suffering from gynecologic problems which permanently will continue to affect her life. She slowly recovered after two years at her father's house. Since she was a married woman, she needed to return to her husband sooner or later. However, when she arrived, she found out that her husband was suffering from PTSD. His father hired a doctor to treat him for the trauma. However, his hands do not stop shaking and he is unable to feed himself, let alone work to support the family. Ever since marrying a husband younger than her, Zhuang Xian Tu had been bearing the responsibilities of household chores and labor at her in-laws. Even if she felt sick as a result of her treatment at the comfort station, she would swallow her pain and press on. Her father in-law soon passed away and her mother in-law remarried, taking all the valuables with her. The young couple lived in a bare house with nothing to live on other than her father's and relatives' support. She also had to do most of the family chores in order to support her family. Her suffering was caused mostly by the Japanese soldiers. In 1998, she arrived in Tokyo hoping to sue Japan for her loss. However, they ruled against compensating her as a victim.